"Are you saying ███████ to get you back i████████ ████

A nod.

"Callie doesn't know, then, that you've already turned me down once before?" he asked in a lowered, private voice.

"It's not that I don't like you, Liam." Kate, usually so sure of herself, sounded off balance with an unsteady shake in her voice.

"That's good to know."

Liam acted on instinct instead of listening to his head. He reached out, took Kate's face in his hands and kissed her on the lips.

It was a short kiss—sweet, gentle, instead of romantic or sensual. But it was a kiss full of promise. It was a kiss that could be his future.

"That's good to know," he said again. "Because I like you, Kate. A whole heck of a lot."

* * *

THE BRANDS OF MONTANA:
Wrangling their own happily-ever-afters

Dear Reader!

Thank you for choosing *A Bride for Liam Brand*, the tenth Special Edition book featuring the Brand family. *A Bride for Liam Brand* continues the saga of the Brand family of Sugar Creek Ranch, located just outside of picturesque Bozeman, Montana.

A Bride for Liam Brand tells the story of large-animal veterinarian Liam Brand and horse trainer Kate King. Liam is a divorced father of two who is considered to be one of the most eligible bachelors of Bozeman. Mothers have been trying to snag Liam for their daughters for years, but Liam, already burned by marriage, is holding out for a once-in-a-lifetime love. When Liam reconnects with Kate, he realizes that the bride he has been dreaming of was right there in Bozeman all along.

Single mother Kate King is the owner of Triple K Ranch, a horse training and breeding facility she inherited from her father. Between managing a Montana ranch and taking care of her eighteen-year-old daughter, Calico, who has Down syndrome, Kate has forgotten all about romance in her own life. But when Kate's regular veterinarian takes ill and Dr. Brand comes out to the Triple K to treat one of her horses, the single mother begins to imagine what her life might be like if she were Liam Brand's bride.

I invite you to visit my website, joannasimsromance.com, and while you're there, be sure to sign up for *Rendezvous Magazine* for Brand-family extras, news and swag. Part of the joy of writing is hearing from readers. If you write me, I will write you back! That's a promise.

Happy reading!

Joanna

A Bride for Liam Brand

Joanna Sims

HARLEQUIN SPECIAL EDITION

Recycling programs
for this product may
not exist in your area.

ISBN-13: 978-1-335-46557-3

A Bride for Liam Brand

Copyright © 2018 by Joanna Sims

Printed in U.S.A.

Joanna Sims is proud to pen contemporary romance for Harlequin Special Edition. Joanna's series, The Brands of Montana, features hardworking characters with hometown values. You are cordially invited to join the Brands of Montana as they wrangle their own happily-ever-afters. And, as always, Joanna welcomes you to visit her at her website: joannasimsromance.com.

Books by Joanna Sims

Harlequin Special Edition

The Brands of Montana

A Wedding to Remember
Thankful for You
Meet Me at the Chapel
High Country Baby
High Country Christmas
A Match Made in Montana

Marry Me, Mackenzie!
The One He's Been Looking For
A Baby for Christmas

Visit the Author Profile page at Harlequin.com for more titles.

Dedicated to my sister, Beth Elaine...
Thank you for being one of my first editors
and shaping the writer I have become.
I love you.

Chapter One

"*Mommy!*"

Callie's scream caused Kate King to drop the heavy Western saddle she was carrying and run toward the sound of her daughter's voice.

"*Mommy!*"

"Callie!" Kate ran down the wide, center aisle of her fifty-stall barn. "Callie!"

The mother and daughter nearly collided when Kate rounded a corner at the end of the long, concrete aisle.

"What's wrong?" Kate put her hands on her daughter's shoulders, giving her face and body a cursory check with her concerned eyes.

Callie's round face was flushed bright red and drenched with tears and sweat. Her daughter was eighteen-years-old, an adult by any standard, but Callie had been born with Down syndrome. Negative emotions, in particular, were difficult for Callie to process.

"Take a minute." Her daughter was gasping for air, struggling to speak. "Catch your breath."

Callie leaned forward a bit, closed her eyes, coughed several times and followed her mother's instructions.

"Visa…" Callie finally got the words out. "He's hurt, Mommy!"

Kate was, at first, relieved that her daughter wasn't the one injured, but the last thing a horse owner wanted to hear was that one of the herd was injured. So, the relief she had originally felt was fleeting.

"It's okay, Callie." Kate gave her daughter a steady look. "Let's go see what's going on with him."

It was just a fact of life that her daughter didn't have many friends in their community; Bozeman, Montana, was a small town surrounded by ranches and uninhabited swaths of land. There simply weren't any other young adults with a similar disability living close by— so every animal on their ranch was Callie's friend. And she took it hard if any of her friends were injured or sick.

Visa, whose registered name was Expense Account, was a rare member of their horse-breeding ranch. The majority of the horses on the Triple K Ranch were Quarter horses with excellent pedigrees. Visa, on the other hand, was a Dutch Warmblood and Hanoverian mix, and he was Callie's favorite.

Together, they walked quickly out to the pasture closest to the barn; each horse had its designated pasture and turnout time. Visa, who wasn't the most assertive horse in the herd, was always turned out with the older, more experienced geldings.

Kate spotted typically social and "in everyone's business" Visa, standing alone and away from the herd. The owner of the Triple K, her brow furrowed with concern, unlatched the gate to the pasture.

"Wait for me here, please, Callie."

"I—I want to help." Her daughter said.

"Callie." Her tone brooked no argument. "This I need you to wait here, please."

Callie, in her own right, was a talented horsewoman; she had been raised working with these elegant creatures and had been riding before she could walk. But, in this moment, Kate didn't want the distraction of watching out for Callie while she tried to figure out what was going on with Visa.

"Hi, good-looking boy," Kate said as she approached Visa. She spoke in a calm soothing voice that she used with all of the horses.

Visa was a beautiful russet-red with black legs and a black mane and tail. The horse, which typically greeted her with a friendly head bump, pinned back its ears at her, gnashed his teeth, and tossed his head aggressively. Visa loved to scratch his face by rubbing his head on her shoulder and arm; his unusual behavior served to underscore the fact that something was wrong.

"Okay. Okay," Kate said in a low, gentle voice, ignoring the pinned ears and his attempts to bite her while she began to take inventory of his physical state. The biggest red flag for her was the fact that he wasn't putting weight on his right hind leg.

"Why are you standing way out here all by yourself?" Kate ran her hand along the young horse's muscular body. "That's not like you."

Careful not to move in a way that would spook Visa,

Kate kept her right hand on his haunch while she bent forward to get a closer look at the hind leg. There was a distinctive gash above Visa's hoof it looked like a crescent, and she immediately suspected that the young gelding had got too nosey with one of the older horses and been kicked for his trouble.

"Easy, Visa. Let me just take a quick look. Did you get kicked?" She ran her hand down the leg; the moment she got near the gash with her fingers, Visa lifted his leg to pull it away from her.

Kate straightened her body, acid beginning to roil in her stomach. A leg injury in a horse was never good news.

"Okay," she said softly to Visa. "Let's see you walk."

The horse trainer hooked her finger into the horse's halter and clucked her tongue to get Visa to walk a step forward. The horse jerked his head, resisting at first, before he agreed to take a couple of steps forward. The second he tried to put weight on that right hind leg, Kate's suspicions were confirmed: Visa was lame. She couldn't know, without an X-ray, how bad the injury was. But there was an undisputable truth of horse ownership—no legs, no horse.

Kate called out to her daughter to fetch her a lead rope. Red-faced and sweaty, Callie handed her the rope.

"I-is he hurt b-bad?"

"I'm not sure, kiddo. Let's get him back to the barn and we'll call Dr. McGee. Do me a favor. Go check Visa's stall and make sure it's been cleaned."

While her daughter rushed back into the barn, lead rope in hand, Kate headed back to Visa.

"This is going to be hard, Visa. But we'll do it together." She clipped the lead rope to the horse's halter and began the painstaking walk back to the barn.

Along the way, the rest of the herd, curious creatures, tried to join them in their journey, but Kate shooed them away. One of Visa's pasture mates had seriously injured him, that much she knew, but she couldn't pinpoint which horse had done the damage.

Callie hurriedly opened the gate so Visa could limp through.

"I-is he going to b-be okay? He looks like he's hurt b-bad." Tears had returned to Callie's brown eyes.

"It might be a broken leg, Callie. I'm not sure." Kate had always told her daughter the truth. "But I do know that we have to be strong for Visa. We have to be calm so he can stay calm. You have to try, okay?"

"Okay," Callie said as she shut the gate behind them. "I—I'll try."

It took a long time to get the lame horse back to his stall; once he was settled, Kate asked Callie to get Visa a pad of hay to keep him occupied while she called her regular vet.

"Oh, Kate," Dr. McGee's receptionist, Dawn, said, "I'm so sorry, but Dr. McGee is out with the flu—sick as a dog, poor man."

Kate shook her head in frustration. Dr. McGee had been her vet for years, and she simply didn't trust anyone else with her horses.

"It sounds like you need someone right away." The receptionist filled in the silence. "I can refer you to Dr. Brand. I have his number right here if you'd like to have it."

Kate had gone to school with Liam Brand, starting in kindergarten. Yes, she grew up with him, and yes, she ran into him every now and again in town. But she had no idea what kind of veterinarian skills Liam Brand had. Unfortunately, she wasn't in a position to question her own vet's referral. Kate took the number, thanked the receptionist for her time and then immediately called Dr. Brand.

"He-*llo*." Liam Brand tapped the green telephone symbol to answer the phone quickly so he could still keep his eyes on the road.

"May I speak with Dr. Brand, please?"

"You got 'im."

"Hi, Dr. Brand. This is Kate King." The woman on the other end of the line paused for a second. "Triple K Ranch?"

Large-animal veterinarian Liam Brand didn't want to let on, but he didn't need any additional qualifiers beyond Kate's name to identify who she was. He was a little old to have a crush, he supposed, but she certainly had caught his interest when their paths had crossed from time to time in the small Montana town of Bozeman. They had known each other all their lives, but Kate wasn't much on small talk with old acquaintances, so he typically admired her from afar.

"How can I help you, Ms. King?"

"Kate," she corrected. "One of my horses turned up lame this morning. Dr. McGee is out sick today, as I'm sure you know by now. I really need someone to come out to the ranch and x-ray Visa's leg. Would you be able to fit me into your schedule? I know it's short notice, but I'd really appreciate it."

Liam already knew that he had back-to-back appointments—it was foaling season, so he was typically booked dawn until dusk.

"I do know about Dr. McGee—I've been getting calls all day from his clients. I'm double booked."

"Dr. Brand." Liam could hear the stress in her voice. "I know you're swamped, but any help you can give me would really be appreciated. It doesn't matter how late you get here." She paused before she added, "Visa is Callie's favorite horse."

The minute Kate mentioned her daughter, Callie, Liam felt that familiar tug on his heartstrings. He'd watched Callie grow over the years; for a while there, before the divorce, his son had attended the same school. She was a special little girl—always smiling, always laughing. If Kate was trying to sway him by mentioning her daughter, it had worked.

After taking a couple of moments to make a decision, Dr. Brand finally said, "Here—let me pull over so I can figure this out."

"Okay. Thank you."

Liam pulled his mobile-vet truck onto the side of the road so he could take a closer look at his schedule. All of his clients were so far apart that driving time made his logjammed schedule even more complicated.

"Let's do this," he finally offered. "I'll come to the Triple K after my last appointment. I'll warn you now— it's gonna be late. After dark, for sure."

"That's not a problem! Whenever you can get here!" Kate exclaimed in a way that made him smile a bit. "I can't thank you enough, Dr. Brand. Truly. Thank you."

As he had predicted, Dr. Liam Brand arrived at the Triple K Ranch after dark. For Kate and Callie, it had been a long day of waiting. When they heard Dr. Brand's truck wheels making a crunching noise on their gravel driveway, both Kate and her daughter abandoned their mucking and jogged to the entrance of the barn to greet Dr. Brand.

"I'm sorry I couldn't get here any sooner," the large-animal vet told her.

"We're just so grateful that you could come." Kate offered her hand. "I know you've already had a long day."

Liam Brand was over six feet tall with a slender physique of a man who took care of his health. His hair, cut short, had turned a dark honey color over the years, which offset, in a very appealing way, the sky blue of his eyes and the golden color of his skin. He was wearing jeans, stained from a day on the job, with the logo of his vet clinic embroidered on the left chest of a light-blue cotton top.

"Hello, Calico." Dr. Brand took the time to acknowledge her daughter.

Liam knew that her daughter's nickname was Callie, but he had always used her formal, given name "Calico" whenever he spoke to her.

Callie smiled shyly at Liam; Kate knew that look in her daughter's large, brown eyes. The young woman developed crushes in the blink of an eye and Liam Brand, Kate observed, was Callie's official new crush.

"Hi," Callie said, ducking her head to the side and gave an embarrassed laugh.

"Let's go see what's going on with Visa," Dr. Brand said after he lifted his rolling mobile-vet kit out of the back of his truck, which had been outfitted with everything a traveling large-animal vet would need to do his or her job.

Dr. Brand wanted to see Visa walk on the concrete; the horse had taken only a few steps before the vet nodded. He asked that they put Visa in cross ties, and then, silently, methodically, with the seriousness Kate appreciated, the vet began his physical exam of the Hanoverian mix. After a thorough exam, Dr. Brand offered some possible diagnoses. The possible culprits for Visa's lameness had all occurred to Kate as well—it could be laminitis, it could be a soft tissue injury, there was a possibility of an abscess in the hoof. But the last possibility that Dr. Brand mentioned, a fracture of the short pastern bone, the bone right above the hoof, was the diagnosis Kate feared the most. Most equine ailments could be healed with the right care and the right perseverance. A fracture? That was a whole different ball of wax. Kate didn't hesitate to agree to get Visa x-rayed.

Kate and Callie stood by Visa's head, offering him encouraging words as the vet set up the portable X-ray machine. If she had wondered about Liam's ability as a veterinarian, watching him now dispelled all of those notions. No, he wasn't as experienced as Dr. McGee, but he was thorough, deliberate and spoke as if he had memorized every textbook he read. While he worked, Liam discussed the recent literature and findings from current research. There wasn't a question she asked him that he didn't answer with the breadth and depth of a man who knew his business. When Liam had as many years of practice under his belt as Dr. McGee, he was going to be a top-notch veterinarian.

Dr. Brand released Visa back to his stall, and by the time Kate returned, the vet was ready to discuss the results of the X-ray. With her arm around Callie's shoulders, as much for her own support as to comfort her daughter, Kate stood close to Dr. Brand so she could see the X-ray of Visa's hind leg projected on the screen. The news wasn't good—she could see that before he even began to point to the hairline fracture in the short pastern bone.

"I-is he going to b-be okay?" Callie already had tears in her eyes; yes, her daughter had a serious intellectual disability, but she understood much more about life than most people would give her credit for.

Kate tightened her arm to hold her daughter to comfort her.

"Well." Dr. Brand's words were measured as he addressed them both. "If Visa was going to have a fracture on his leg, this is the best place to do it."

She had been holding her breath again; Kate told herself to keep on breathing. She was fully expecting Liam to tell her that Visa, only five and so young, would have to be put down.

"If you keep him on stall rest for two months, I can come back and take another X-ray to see if he's done some healing," Dr. Brand said. "Of course, Dr. McGee would be able to help you with that, as well."

Kate took a second to process the information before she replied, "You've started with him. I'd feel better if you just stayed with this case."

"I'd be happy to do it."

All three of them turned to walk in the direction of the vet's truck; Kate already had her checkbook in her back pocket to pay.

"How much do we owe you?"

"I don't really handle that part of the deal. Go ahead

and call the office tomorrow. Ask for Irene—she handles all the billing." He pulled a card out of the console of his truck and handed it to her. "She'll take care of you."

"Okay," Kate said, surprised that Liam didn't take payment on the spot. "Are you sure?"

"Yep." Liam opened one of the storage lockers built onto the back of his truck.

"Do you like chili?" Callie asked the vet.

"Sure do." Dr. Brand loaded his mobile kit into the locker.

Kate liked that Liam didn't disregard her daughter—he included her, he looked at her directly and spoke to her like she had value.

"Do you want to have chili with us? That's what we're having for dinner."

Kate hadn't expected her daughter to extend a dinner invitation to Liam; even more unexpected was her own follow-up to Callie's invitation.

"We have plenty," she told Liam. "It's the least we could do. I'm sure you skipped dinner so you could come out here."

Liam didn't say yes or no as he loaded his equipment into his truck.

"Do you like orange or grape soda?" Callie asked Liam. "Which do you want?"

Kate put her hand on her daughter's shoulder. "He hasn't accepted your invitation yet."

Liam locked the back of his truck. "I like grape."

For the briefest of seconds, Liam caught Kate's eye, and she saw something so strong and kind in those blue eyes that she had to remind herself to look away.

"I—I like grape, too!" Callie told the vet excitedly,

as if she had just discovered that they had something very special in common.

Her daughter spun around and headed off in the direction of their modest ranch-style house with the new steel roof and fresh coat of moss green paint.

"I'm sorry," Kate told him when her daughter was out of earshot. "I hope she didn't put you on the spot."

"I'm hungry, and all I've got in my icebox is a piece of suspicious cheese and condiments." Liam adjusted his long legs so he could keep pace with her.

Kate cracked a smile. "Well, then, I'm glad she invited you."

She caught Liam staring at her profile. "I don't usually say yes. But we're talking about chili and grape soda. An offer like that doesn't come up every day."

It had been a long day for Liam Brand; he was grateful and honored that a man like Dr. McGee—a man he admired—would send his clients to him when he was out sick. But the 50 percent increase in appointments, which entailed juggling his already booked days with Dr. McGee's overflow, had put him under the gun and way behind. He was exhausted—and he usually wasn't exhausted. If it had been anyone other than Kate King and Callie who invited him in for dinner, he would have gracefully declined and headed home.

"We weren't expecting anyone," Kate told him as she picked up random items on the way to the kitchen.

The King home was cozy and lived-in. The outside of the house had some updating recently, but the inside was like stepping back in time to the 1970s. Kate was known in the greater Bozeman area as one of the best horse trainers and breeders in the state of Montana. Her techniques for training horses and riders in a humane manner was the stuff of legends; on the other hand, homemaking did not seem to be much of a priority. The furniture hadn't been updated since Kate was a kid. In fact, Liam remembered sitting on that same forest green and navy blue plaid couch back when he was in elementary school one summer when his father came out to the Triple K to buy some new horses from Kate's father. It was obvious that every bit of her heart, her soul, her time and her money went to taking care of her daughter and her horses. That was her love, and he could appreciate that about her because that was exactly how he felt about life: family and horses mattered more than stainless-steel appliances and granite countertops.

"Something smells mighty good in here." Liam sat at the small kitchen island with the sunshine-yellow laminate countertop.

What the King house lacked in decor, it more than made up for it in the homey feel and a tantalizing aroma permeating the kitchen.

"Grandpa taught me." Callie lifted the lid off the large pot on the stove.

"I didn't know you were the chef of the family," Liam said to Kate's daughter.

"Callie is the only chef in this house," Kate gave her daughter a quick hug from behind. "Thank goodness she loves to cook, or we'd both starve. Isn't that true, kiddo?"

Callie nodded seriously. "That is true. I-I have saved us from starving."

Liam sat at Kate King's counter, watching the horse trainer interact with her daughter, while he gulped down grape soda, which he hadn't had since he was a kid.

This visit to the Triple K Ranch was an unexpected blast into his past.

Every time he emptied a can of soda, Callie would put another cold can of it in front of him. He didn't even have to ask. It had been a long time since Liam felt like he was part of a family; he'd been separated for several years, and the divorce had finally been settled the year before. The judge had granted full, physical custody of their two children to his ex-wife and liberal visitation to him; now he was a long-distance father to two teenagers. His son and daughter lived in Seattle, Washington, with his ex-wife and her new husband. Although he had known that his ex-wife, Cynthia, had been dating during their separation, it had still been a shock when she remarried so quickly after the divorce had been finalized. He hated being a video-chat father and a "see you on your next school break" dad. But, that fight was over and he had lost—big time.

He'd always been the kind of man who wanted to be married, to have kids, to make a home with a woman. But it hadn't worked out that way. Liam had his work— his salvation—and a big family with lots of siblings, yet he always went home to an empty house. He liked being in Kate King's house, chitchatting and laughing about nothing in particular while Calico stirred the chili and put an extra place setting on the table.

Once Callie announced that she was ready to serve, Liam joined them at their little square table, wobbly on its legs, and hungrily dived into the large bowl of chili. Perhaps he shouldn't have been so shocked at how good the chili was—perhaps he underestimated Callie because of her disability—but Callie's chili was incredible.

Two bowls later, Liam was completely stuffed and wishing he hadn't been so greedy. He felt more like curling up on Kate's old plaid couch than driving forty-five minutes back to his family's ranch, Sugar Creek.

"That was the best chili I've ever had," he told Kate's daughter. "Hand's down. The best."

Callie smiled shyly with pleasure, sometimes finding it difficult to look him in the eye.

As she picked up his bowl to take it to the sink, Callie said, "I-I'm making steak and garlic mashed potatoes tomorrow night."

Liam smiled at her. "I'm sure that's going to be another masterpiece of a meal, Calico."

She stood by his chair, his bowl in hand. "Do you want to come for dinner tomorrow?"

Liam saw Kate's expression, fleeting as it was; she had no idea Callie would invite him for a second dinner, and she wasn't on board with the idea. Kate sanitized her expression quickly as she said, "Callie, I'm sure Dr. Brand can't come out all this way just for dinner."

"Actually—" he didn't plan it; the words just popped out of his mouth "—I think that steak and garlic mashed potatoes are *definitely* worth the drive. What time's dinner?"

Chapter Two

"I still don't know *what* possessed you to invite Dr. Brand for dinner tonight, Callie!" Kate said as she was attempting to stuff a family pack of paper towels onto the top shelf of her pantry.

"He likes my cooking."

Kate had been irritated all day about their dinner guest. She was annoyed with her daughter for extending the invitation, and she was even more annoyed with Liam for accepting.

"Everyone loves your cooking." She shoved the paper towels hard with both hands.

Callie put her hand over her mouth and giggled. "True."

No matter how hard she shoved that stupid pack of paper towels, it refused to fit into the space. Kate stared at the offending paper towels before she sighed, grabbed ahold of the plastic encasing the paper towels and yanked on it until she pulled it free and dropped it onto the floor.

"We don't have company during the week." She picked up the paper towels and put them on top of the refrigerator.

"I—I know." Her daughter was busy gathering the ingredients she would need to make dinner. Callie always needed help with measuring, but she could follow her list of ingredients and then double-check after she was done. "B-but," her daughter said as if she were the parent, "you're gonna need someone to eat dinner with when I—I'm living in New York."

This had been a conversation that had been going on for years. In spite of her disability, Callie was a very goal-oriented young woman. She wanted to live in New York City on her own, go to culinary school and then open a restaurant. Kate had always supported Callie's dreams, but there had to be limits.

"You know that New York isn't an option, Callie. Our life is here at the Triple K."

"That's why I—I'm going without you." Her daughter put her armful of ingredients on the counter. "You stay here, and I—I go to New York."

This was said with another giggle.

Kate walked up behind her daughter, wrapped her arms around her shoulders and kissed her on the cheek. "I love you, sweet girl."

Always affectionate ever since she was a baby, Callie turned in her arms and hugged her tightly. "Don't be afraid, Mommy. I—I'll be okay."

"If you want to move out, Callie, you know I support that. But you've got to take baby steps. Get a place in town."

"I-I'll live in New York first."

This wasn't the first, or last, discussion about New York. Down syndrome hadn't quelled Callie's ability to dream big for herself; she was goal-oriented and ambitious, dreaming of attending culinary school in New York City. For someone born with Down syndrome, Callie was on the higher end of the spectrum as far as her IQ was concerned, but there would never be a time when she could live independently in a small town like Bozeman, much less in the largest city in the country. Her daughter was so full of life, so full of dreams, but simple, daily tasks, like taking money out of an ATM machine, stumped Callie.

It was important to Kate that her daughter gain as much independence as possible; they had often spoken about Callie finding an apartment in town. Kate had even been in touch with a local, non-profit organization that supported individuals with disabilities to review options for transitional living in Bozeman. But every time they discussed moving, Callie inevitably circled back to her goal of moving to the Big Apple.

"You may move out and hate it," Kate teased her daughter.

"No." Callie said, emphatically. "I-I know what I want."

She waited for Callie to slowly go over the ingredient list, check each item off as she doubled-checked to make certain she had everything she needed. Her daughter leaned her elbows on the counter, her face very close to the enlarged print on the recipe card, talking aloud to herself as she went along. It had taken years to develop this routine, this step toward independent life, and Kate was proud to watch Callie make continued progress. Her daughter had gotten the King stubbornness and determination quite honestly.

"I—I'm ready," Callie told her.

Kate stayed with Callie, making sure all of her measurements were accurate, before she headed back to the barn. The barn, the ranch, was both her albatross and her solace. When she was angry or upset, there was nothing better for it than mucking out stalls. But the work was never ending and there was always something that needed to be fixed.

"Well, Visa." She had ended hours of work back at the injured horse's stall. Now that he was stall bound, she spent more time with him. He was a young horse and to be stuck in a twelve by twelve space for months was going to be tough for him.

Kate rubbed the space between Visa's eyes, then twirled his long, black forelock around her finger.

"Guess who's coming for dinner?" The horse trainer frowned at the thought.

Halfway through her work, she had thought to call Liam and give him a chance to get off the hook. But in the end, she thought better of it. Liam was a smart man; he'd figure out that she was trying to revoke her daughter's invitation. No, if he wanted out, he'd let her know. She knew that she had a reputation in Bozeman for being private and a bit standoffish, but no one could legitimately pin rudeness on her and she'd like to keep it that way. All she could really do was hope that Liam's schedule would prevent him from coming all the way out to the Triple K. The rest of the afternoon, while she paid bills in the office above the barn, Kate hoped that her phone would ring. But often times, hoping wasn't enough to make something happen.

"Howdy!" Liam Brand had been looking forward to heading out to the Triple K all day.

In fact, the day didn't seem to go by fast enough.

"Hi, Dr. Brand." Kate was kneeling at the front of the barn, surrounded by a pride of ragtag barn cats who had seen better days.

Liam sensed that the horse trainer was still in the process of warming up to the idea of him having dinner at her ranch for the second night in a row; even when she wasn't smiling, with the light of a smile reaching her eyes, Liam still thought she was mighty pretty.

"I'd appreciate you callin' me Liam." He stopped a few feet away from her. "We go back an awful long way."

Instead of responding, Kate finished feeding her barn cats. "I have to have the oldest barn cats ever. I've got to feed them now—they're too old to catch mice anymore."

Liam laughed. Kate's cats were bony from old age, with noticeable cataracts, scraggly fur and weak meows. One brown tabby cat with narrow shoulders, curled white whiskers and a barrel belly broke away from the group to greet him. Her scratchy meow touched his heart as he knelt to pet her.

"Sissy." Kate glanced up from her chore. "She's the flirt of the barn."

The old feline rubbed her face and body against Liam's knee, purring hard and loud, before falling onto her side at his feet. Sissy gave him a slow blink, a sign of love from a cat, while her paws curled under happily.

"Love has always been more important to her than food."

Liam petted the retired mouser until the feline decided it was, indeed, time to fill her belly. Kate stood and he joined her. They watched the ex-mousers make short work of the food she had put down for them.

"I can't seem to get her eyes cleared up," Kate said after a minute or two. "They're always so swollen. Allergies, I suppose."

"I'll give you one of the ointments I like to use with cats before I leave."

"Thanks." She seemed surprised when she said, "I'd really appreciate that."

Liam wanted to check on his patient, swinging by Visa's stall before he strode beside Kate back to the house. It occurred to him, as he walked next to the horse trainer, that he didn't have to measure his stride. She had some long legs of her own, and it was nice to walk beside her.

"Look who I found!" Kate said to her daughter when they entered the small ranch house.

"Hi, Dr. Brand!" Callie immediately met them just inside the door and hugged him in that friendly way of hers.

"It smells mighty good in here again, Calico," Liam told the young lady.

"She's been cooking all day." Kate shut the door.

"I've been thinking about your cookin' all day," he said.

"I hope you brought your appetite," the pretty rancher said. "I think my daughter cooked for ten."

"Trust me." He took his place at the kitchen island. "I brought my appetite."

For the second night in a row, Liam sat in the King home and felt right at home. He liked watching the mother and daughter, so close in their relationship, work together to get ready for dinner. Now that it was his second time sitting at their dinner table, Kate handed him a stack of plates with the silverware so he could help set the table. That gesture alone made him feel even more "a part of it."

They sat down together, held hands for a prayer, and then Liam dug into the incredible fare Callie had prepared. He didn't stop eating even when he began to feel stuffed. The only time he got this kind of cooking was any Sunday he made it out to the family ranch for breakfast. Home-cooked dinners were far and few between for him. So was the conversation they had during dinner. It had been a long time since he had someone to share his day with, talk about his passion of caring for animals. Kate got it. They weren't exactly in the same business, but the animals on her ranch were more than just part of her business—they were part of her family.

"I'll have Callie fix you some leftovers," Kate said with a laugh. She must have noticed him still eyeing the food on the table after had already filled his plate twice.

"Are you sure?"

The horse trainer smiled at him again, and this time the smile reached her eyes. "I'm sure. It'll give the chef an excuse to cook something new tomorrow. Isn't that right, Callie?"

The young woman nodded, but her attention was distracted by the sound of a video call coming in on a tablet on the counter. Kate's daughter jumped up, ran to the counter looked at the screen and then squealed with excitement.

"I-it's Tony!" Callie snatched the tablet off the counter, accepted the call and hurried down the narrow hallway leading to the three small bedrooms at the back of the house.

Kate sighed, staring after her daughter.

"Tony?"

She stared down the hallway a moment longer before she responded. Kate's shoulders lifted ever so slightly. Was it a sign of frustration or resignation? He couldn't be sure.

"Callie's boyfriend. They met in an online support group for young adults with Down syndrome. If I had known this was going to happen, I'm not sure I would have been so excited to sign her up."

That shocked him. Just like Callie's amazing talent in the kitchen, it hadn't crossed his mind that she would have a boyfriend.

They began to clear the table with the sound of Callie's laughter and excited talking drifting down the hall.

"Serious?" He put the last dish on the counter.

Kate breathed in deeply and sighed again. She tucked a couple of wayward hairs behind her ear, a gesture he'd seen her do many times that night. "I think she's taking it way too seriously. She thinks she's in love."

Liam stood at the sink, turned on the water and waited for it to get hot.

"You don't have to do that." She frowned at the running water.

"I've got this." He wasn't ready to get kicked out just yet.

While he rinsed the dishes and loaded the dishwasher, Kate fixed him containers of leftovers, giving him the lion's share of the rest of the food.

"So, you think being in love is a bad thing?" He asked his hostess.

"No." Kate frowned at the question. "I don't. But Callie doesn't always see the big picture. She thinks that what she sees in the movies is what love is all about. That's not real life."

"No. It's not. Marriage is hard work."

And he was living proof that hard work wasn't enough to sustain a marriage.

Kate sent him what he assumed was a sympathetic look, dispelling any notion that news of his divorce hadn't spread all over the small town.

"Relationships, in general, are hard," she said.

"Well, Calico is mighty lucky to have you to help her navigate through life."

Kate laughed as she snapped the Tupperware lid into place. "Trust me. My daughter has grown weary of my advice."

"That's about as typical as it gets, isn't it?"

"Yes." That made Kate smile. "I suppose it is."

They didn't talk much after that, and that was okay with him. Kate wasn't chatty—she was quiet, inward in her thoughts, and even though he'd like for her to open up to him, he wasn't in any hurry. He had a feeling that if he wanted to get to know Kate better, he was going to have to work the long game.

"Coffee?" she asked him. "For the road?"

He knew that was her not-so-subtle way of letting him know that it was time for him to begin to be on his way.

"I could sure use a cup. I'm fighting the desire to take a nap on your couch."

He'd gotten her to smile more than once tonight—

he was making some progress. Kate had always been focused, determined and serious, even when they were in high school, but she seemed to have lost some of her joy. Had he even heard her laugh?

"Mommy!" Callie came bounding into the kitchen clutching the tablet to her chest. The young lady, her brown eyes shining, her round cheeks flushed, spun around in a circle, giggling happily.

"Do I even need to ask how the phone call went?" Kate brushed back her daughter's hair and then put her hands on her Callie's shoulders.

"He asked me to be his date for the dance!" Callie told her mom excitedly, giving a little jump. "I can't wait!"

"Callie," Kate said gently, but seriously, "you know we can't go this year. We talked about this."

The young woman's face fell. "*You* can't go. Why can't I—I go? I—I'm old enough. I—I can go *b-by myself.*"

Callie started to cry; Kate brushed her daughter's tears away with her thumbs, her eyes soft with under-standing and something else—sadness.

"Callie, we have company," she said. "We'll talk about this later. Okay?"

"Okay." Callie frowned. "B-but I-I'm old enough to go b-by myself!"

The young woman stomped out of the living room, down the narrow hallway, and slammed the door to her bedroom.

Liam and Kate took a cup of coffee out to the porch and sat on the porch swing, with the warm summer air filled with the sound of crickets and a night owl howl-ing in the distance.

"I appreciate you indulging me." He held up the coffee cup. He was actually too tired to think about driving the nearly hour home.

Kate nodded as she took a sip of her own coffee.

After a moment of staring after her daughter, Kate said with a sigh, "Sorry about earlier. It's the annual Down syndrome conference. I try to take her every year. Now that Tony is going, missing it is going to be tough for her."

"No need to apologize." Liam tried to reassure his hostess. "Love is serious business."

"That's true. But Callie's disability makes all of this so much harder to navigate." Kate tucked her hair behind her ear. "I never even thought about a boyfriend when she was growing up. Now she wants to get married. Have babies."

"I suppose that's natural," Liam said after a second of thinking it over. The fact that Kate was talking to him so openly about her daughter was a welcome surprise. He didn't want to screw it up by saying something stupid or unintentionally insensitive. He wanted to find a way to be a part of Kate's and Callie's lives.

"Yes," she agreed, holding her warm cup with both hands. "But Callie is never going to be able to live on her own."

"She seems really independent."

Kate sent him the smallest of smiles. "She is. Everyone with Down syndrome is different, just like the rest of us. We were lucky—Callie's intelligence is higher on the range. But..." Kate frowned into her coffee cup. "She'll never be able to live without support, and no matter how many times we talk about it, I just can't get her to understand. She wants to move to New York

City and go to culinary school and open a restaurant. She also wants to move to California, marry Tony and start having babies. In her mind, it's possible to do both, at the same time."

"I wish my daughter were that ambitious," he interjected, and he meant it.

"Callie is ambitious." Kate nodded. "She has so many dreams and goals—none of them here in Montana.

They finished their coffee, and when they went back into the house, Callie, seemingly recovered from her outburst, gave him a big hug when he came into the kitchen to put his coffee cup in the sink and pick up his leftovers. This time when Callie asked him to dinner for the next night, he declined. He couldn't keep on accepting the daughter's invitation to be able to spend time with the mother.

"I appreciate you letting me come on out tonight." Liam put the containers in the front seat of his truck.

"Callie invited you."

He shut the door to his truck and then stood in front of the trainer; her arms were crossed in front of her body.

Liam chuckled. "I was waiting all day for you to uninvite me."

The half-moon was putting off enough light for him to see a fleeting expression of guilt flash across her face.

"I wouldn't do that."

Liam ducked his head, putting it just a little closer to hers. "Admit it, though. You thought about it."

Kate turned her face away from him, her lips pressed together as if she wanted to stop herself from admitting it. Then, unexpectedly, she laughed.

"I'm sorry." She looked into his face then. "I'm not much on company."

He didn't say anything, because he sensed she had more to say.

"Callie wants me to start dating again…"

Their eyes met and Liam felt a spark. He felt it, and he was pretty sure that Kate felt it too.

"Are you saying I'm part of some evil plan to get you back into the dating game?"

A nod.

"Calico doesn't know, then, that you've already turned me down once before?" he asked in a lowered, private voice.

Kate took a small step back, but he wasn't going to let her get off the hook that easily. He took a small step forward.

"It's not that I don't like you, Liam." Kate, usually so sure of herself, sounded off balance with a shake in her voice.

"That's good to know."

In that moment, in the soft moonlight, Liam acted on instinct instead of listening to his head. He reached out, took Kate's face in his hands and kissed her on the lips.

It was a short kiss—sweet, gentle, instead of romantic or sensual. But that kiss was a kiss full of promise. It was a kiss that could be his future.

Surprised, Kate stepped backward again. His hands fell away from her face and they stood there, quietly, staring at each other.

"That's good to know," he said again, "because I like you, Kate. A whole heck of a lot."

Chapter Three

"He actually *kissed* me," Kate whispered into the phone. She was in bed, but she wasn't ready for sleep. She had brushed her teeth and then stood in the bathroom staring at the lips that Liam Brand had just *kissed* without any warning or invitation.

"Good for him," her friend Lorrie told her.

Lorrie also had a child with Down syndrome, a little girl much younger than Callie. Lorrie had started an organization to connect parents in Gallatin County and ever since they had worked together to establish an annual, one-mile Buddy Walk in Bozeman to raise awareness and inclusion for people with DS.

"Good?"

"Yes," Lorrie reiterated. "Good. He listened to my advice."

Now Kate sat upright in bed. "What advice was that?"

Lorrie stopped to say something to one of her kids before answering. "He was here to give Dude and Max their shots. He might have mentioned that he was interested in you."

"And?"

"*And* I told him that he'd have to be unconventional. That's all."

Kate couldn't think of a response right away. Her mouth popped open, and she shook her head before she said, "So, you encouraged him to assault me?"

"Okay—now that's way dramatic. All he did was give you a kiss. Tell me you didn't enjoy it. Liam is handsome, smart, *nice* and he's one of the most eligible bachelors in Montana."

"That's not the point." Kate flopped back into the pillows. "I have Callie and the ranch."

"I do know." Lorrie said kindly. "I do. But, just because we have children with special needs doesn't mean we can just put our lives on a shelf. Callie is an adult now, Kate. She needs your help—she'll always need your help—but you're going to have to find something else to do with your life other than focusing all of your attention on Callie. Why not shift some of that focus onto someone like Dr. Brand?"

Quiet for a moment of thought, Kate couldn't deny her friend's logic. Had she been holding Callie back, in part, because her daughter had always been the center of her world? Was she holding Callie back for her own sake? Part of her, deep down, knew that it was, at least, possible.

They talked for another twenty minutes before

they hung up. Lorrie was one of the few people who genuinely understood her struggles with Callie, from fighting for services in the school system, accessing appropriate health care, and the feeling of isolation that could creep in with so many miles between families in a similar situation. She trusted Lorrie; they told each other the unvarnished truth. Her friend had a point. It was time for her to begin to find a new center of her life. Callie was growing up.

"Good morning, Kate." Dawn from Dr. McGee's office had called her out of the blue. "How are you today?"

"I'm good. Just doing barn work, as usual."

"Well, I won't be keepin' you too long." There was something in Dawn's voice that signaled that this wasn't going to be a positive call. "But I do have to share with you that Dr. McGee is going to be retiring."

Up until that point, Kate had been holding the phone between her shoulder and cheek while she continued to muck the stall she was working on. The news made Kate put her pitchfork down; she stood upright and held the phone to her ear with her hand as the receptionist continued.

"He's given me permission to tell all of his longtime clients that he's having some serious health problems and he has to retire."

Kate felt her chest tighten—she loved Dr. McGee. She'd known him since she was a kid and had always assumed that he would keep on working until he took his last breath.

"I'm so sorry to hear that."

"So are we." The receptionist sounded as if she was choking back tears. "It's a...shock."

After she hung up the phone, the weight of the phone call began to hit Kate. Beyond the sadness she was feeling in her heart, and the fact that she was going to have to break the news to Callie, who was crazy about Dr. McGee, what was she going to do about her horses? She had a huge barn to run and having a vet was essential to the health of the horses in her care.

Kate finished mucking out the stall, pushed the cart away from the stall, dropped the pitchfork into the cart and then walked outside to think. It was a blue sky day, not one cloud, and it was warm, just how she liked it. Hands on her hips, Kate ran several ideas through her head before she finally landed on her first move.

"I'll be upstairs in the office if you need me," Kate told two of her regular stable hands. Whenever she conducted business, she liked to sit at her desk in the office above the barn. Sitting at her desk now, with the view of the flat expanse of the pastures abutting the mountains in the background, Kate was always reminded that she was blessed to be living in paradise. But even paradise came with a price.

"He-*llo*."

The way Liam answered his phone always made her smile.

"Hi, Dr. Brand. It's Kate."

"Hi, Kate King," Liam greeted her enthusiastically. "So, we're back to Dr. Brand, are we?"

Kate touched her fingers to her lips, the lips this man had kissed several nights before. It was a kiss, so fleeting, that hadn't been far from her mind.

"This is a business call."

"And here I thought you had finally come to your senses and were calling to ask me out on a date."

He was teasing her—at least in part, he was—and it took her a moment to catch up with him. He had a way of catching her off guard with his humor and his kisses. He spoke before she had a chance to regroup.

"I'm thinkin' that this call is about Dr. McGee retiring?"

"Yes." The words came out of the blue, but the minute Liam echoed the news, Kate felt tears, unbidden, fill her eyes and fall onto her cheeks.

Not wanting Liam to hear her crying, Kate quickly wiped off her cheeks, steeled herself against the sadness she was feeling and focused on the business at hand.

"I've obviously been beaten to the punch," she added.

"Look, Kate." Liam said, his voice reassuringly strong and steady. "If you need me, I'm gonna be there for you. So you can take that worry right off your shoulders."

Relieved, she dropped her head into her hand. "Thank you. You know how important it is to have a support system in place."

"I do," Liam said. "That's what I'm here for."

Their phone call was cut short, making Kate wish that they had more time—he had arrived at his next client and she was hosting a clinic for a group of owners and horses. But just from that brief phone call, Liam had made her feel better. She felt that it was going to be easier to face her day without the worry about who she was going to call if one of the horses in her charge took ill or got injured. Now she knew that she could call Dr. Brand. Liam.

* * *

When word got out that Dr. McGee, a most beloved fixture in the Bozeman area horse scene, was retiring, it wasn't long before a retirement party was organized. Kate, who didn't typically take the time out of her business life to go to parties, carved time out of her schedule to attend. Callie and Kate washed up, put on some clean jeans and boots, and then loaded into one of the King Ranch trucks to head into town.

"I should drive." Callie always said the same thing when they headed off King property. Callie drove, under supervision, on the ranch and, since they owned thousands of acres, she had plenty of dirt roads to drive. But she hadn't been able to pass the driver's license test that would allow her to drive off property and her daughter couldn't seem to accept it.

"You know what I love about you, Calico?" Kate pulled onto the road that would take them into Bozeman.

"Everything?" Callie laughed with a broad smile.

"That's right." Kate reached over and squeezed her daughter's arm. "Everything."

They arrived at The Baxter Downtown, a venue often used in Bozeman for weddings, special events and, in this case, a retirement party. Dr. McGee's wife and staff had reserved the Wilson Suite, a smaller, cozier room accented with dark wood fit for a dignified man.

"Dr. McGee isn't going to like all of this fuss," Kate whispered to her daughter. "At least on the surface."

So many people gathered in the small space while Dr. McGee sat at the head table with his wife and closest staff members; she knew the man well enough to know that he was touched by the turnout, even though she had heard him blustering about all of his friends acting like he was about to be pushing-up daisies when he wasn't ready to go quietly into that good night just yet.

"Is this seat taken?"

The minute Kate heard the sound of Liam's voice, her body responded in the most unusual way. Her heart started to beat a little faster, and the hair on the back of her neck stood up.

"No." Kate found herself smiling at the handsome vet. "Be our guest."

Callie jumped out of her chair and threw her arms around Liam. "Hi, Dr. B-Brand!"

Kate watched Liam closely—he treated her daughter with so much respect and dignity, every time, that she couldn't deny that this was a part of this new feeling she was experiencing for the man.

"Hi, Calico." Liam started to take the seat on the other side of her daughter, but Callie shook her head and sat down in the chair instead.

"You should sit next to Mommy."

"Callie." Kate glanced around quickly, knowing that people were paying attention. "Let Dr. Brand sit where he wants."

"Okay," Callie said sullenly.

Liam took a moment, waited for the mother and daughter to negotiate the situation before he took the seat between them.

He leaned over to say, in that low, baritone voice of his, "This is where I wanted to sit."

Kate wasn't someone who embarrassed easily; she was a woman in a world still dominated by men. But she felt her cheeks grow hot, and she knew that if anyone was watching her face closely, the pleasure she felt by that simple comment was right there in her eyes and the small smile on her lips.

Two of the biggest gossips in Bozeman were sitting directly across from them at the banquet table. The Mendelsohn widows, Beatrice and Emma, were very interested in the new "dynamic" of the handsome eligible veterinarian and the relationship-skittish horse trainer.

"How long have the two of you been courting?" Beatrice got straight to the point.

"We aren't." Kate crinkled her brow a bit. Was it that obvious that she felt "something" akin to happy nerves sitting next to Liam?

"Not yet," Liam added after he took a large sip of his water without ice.

"They make a very handsome couple," Emma told her sister.

"They do," Beatrice agreed. "Very handsome."

"Everyone always said that about John and I," Emma continued. "That we were a handsome couple. Of course, Beatrice was always the prettier one of the two of us. But even my sister has had to admit that my John was the most handsome man—so tall and straight."

Beatrice put down her teacup with a small smile. "Don't pay a bit of attention to Emma. I've never admitted to such a thing."

Emma raised her eyebrows at her sister, puckered her lips a bit and then turned her attention back to them. "You make a very handsome couple. I approve of this match."

"As do I." Her sister agreed loudly enough for the people seated at the table behind them to hear.

Kate and Liam exchanged a quick look, both of them understanding that to make any more denials that they weren't an "item" would only give the sisters more fodder for their gossip. So they both just nodded and smiled, and let the conversation naturally drift in a different direction.

The speeches given by the staff at Dr. McGee's clinic were emotional; even though Kate didn't show it on the outside, she felt such sadness that this amazing man was leaving the profession before his time. Mrs. McGee spoke and then by unanimous applause, Dr. McGee agreed to say a word or two.

"I don't know what's wrong with all of you," Dr. McGee said in a gruff voice laced with an unusual undertone of emotion. "I'm not dead yet. But since y'all are probably the same folks who might make it to my funeral one day, this gets you off the hook for that shindig."

That was the entire speech. That was Dr. McGee. After that brief speech, everyone started to leave. Liam stood, pulled out Callie's chair first, and just as she was pushing back her own chair, she saw the vet reach out his hand to her.

Kate looked at that hand for a split second; it was such a small thing, taking an offered hand, but it seemed like a big deal to her.

Her hand slipped so easily into his—his hand, strong, rough from clinical work in the field, was a perfect fit for hers. She had big hands for a woman, and whenever she held hands with a man, as rare as that was, she always felt like the "dude." With Liam, she felt like a woman holding the hand of a man.

They walked out together, the three of them, and Kate hated the feel of curious eyes on them. It was such a small town that no doubt word had gotten out that

Liam had sat at her table two nights in a row and now they were sitting together at Dr. McGee's retirement party. Gossip was a pastime for some in their town.

"You like Mommy, don't you?" Callie asked Liam when they reached their truck.

Liam, as he always did, took Callie's questions seriously, answered them directly. "Yes, Calico. I do."

Kate sighed at her daughter's question. Callie was Callie, and no matter how many discussions they had about "polite questions," there were just some things that her daughter wasn't going to be able to change.

Callie giggled at Liam's response, turning her head and covering her mouth with her hand.

"Do you want to come over for dinner tonight?" Her daughter threw out of invitation before she got into the truck.

Liam looked directly into Kate's eyes before he said to Callie, "I really appreciate the invite, I really do. I'd love to eat some more of your good cookin,' but the next time I come over for dinner, it's gonna have to be your mom who invites me."

That could have been a moment for her to invite him, but she just wasn't ready. She was feeling things for Liam—she was—and he hadn't been subtle about his attraction to her. But this was territory that hadn't been explored in over a decade! Kate wasn't the type of woman to make drastic changes in her life; she was a tugboat, not a speedboat.

"It was nice spending lunch with you," Kate said, after she climbed behind the wheel.

"Likewise." Liam had a way of looking at her in a way that no other man had in a very long time. Maybe not ever. It was as if he liked everything he saw when he looked at her face.

"I'm sad about Dr. McGee," she admitted to him.

"So am I." Liam had one hand tucked into a front pocket and the other holding her open door. "I could work a lifetime and not feel like half the vet that man is."

"I don't know about that," Kate objected. "I was really impressed with how you handled Visa."

Liam nodded and then shut the door for her. "I appreciate that. I hope to see you again real soon. You too Calico!"

They said their goodbyes then, and she drove away. In the rearview mirror, she saw Liam still standing in the parking lot watching them as they left.

"Mommy! Why didn't you tell him he could come over for dinner?"

"I don't know." Kate told her daughter. But that wasn't entirely true. There was something there between them—she felt it and she could tell that Liam could feel it too. It was something real, something tangible. And it genuinely scared the crap out of her.

A couple of days after Liam had seen Kate and Callie at Dr. McGee's party, he had really struggled with his next move. He could tell that Kate felt the same attraction to him that he did with her. But he could also see that she wasn't ready to jump into a relationship. If he wanted to explore his feelings for Kate, he was going to have to be strategic. Instead of calling, which he wanted to do, he decided to just give her some time to mull over the lunch, and the *kiss*, they had shared.

"He-*llo*!"

It was Kate King on the line.

"I can't believe I forgot about this," the trainer told him. "But I have a prepurchase vet check scheduled for tomorrow. The woman's coming in from Helena, and she's already called several vets…"

"I think she may have called me already," Liam told her.

"She did. I know this is a big ask—but I'm really in a bind. The prospective buyer has no flexibility in her schedule."

When he first got the call from the woman out of Helena, she had mentioned the King Ranch, but his scheduled was still overflowing because of Dr. Mc-Gee's sudden retirement. Thankfully there were a couple of other vets in the area who were able to step up their game.

"I just can't get out there today, Kate. I would if I could," he said, and then added in the silence that followed, "I hope you know that."

"No. I know," Kate told him, her disappointment obvious to him. "I appreciate it."

After another moment of odd silence, she asked, "Could you come out tonight? I know it's a lot to ask, but the indoor riding ring has lights. We ride at night here all the time."

She continued in a lowered voice. "Please, Liam. She's a really big connection for me. If I get this deal done, there could be so much business for the Triple K." After another pause, she added, "I really need this."

The worry he heard in her voice convinced him that he had to find a way to help her. "Okay."

"Okay?"

"I'll be there. As soon as I can. It won't be until six or seven. I already know that for sure."

"Whenever you can get here. I'll let the buyer know," Kate said. "And, Dr. Brand… Liam…I can't thank you enough."

He was already exhausted when he parked his truck in front of Kate's barn. The prospective buyer, a rather fancy-looking woman with platinum hair who was originally from Oklahoma, greeted him with Kate at her side. He was lucky that the exam was uncomplicated—the horse was sound, had good hooves, and had negative flexion tests and X-rays. Although a prepurchase vet check could take up to four hours, this exam went smoothly and he was wrapping up with the potential owner after two hours.

"You shouldn't have any difficulty using this horse for the purposes you've stated," he said to the client. "I should have a report to you by tomorrow afternoon. I won't be able to get it out tonight."

"Tomorrow will be just fine." The woman with the heavy Oklahoma accent smiled at him.

Liam packed up his equipment, while Kate showed the woman to her car. They met back at his truck just as he was finished loading.

With a sigh, Kate, in cutoff shorts that showed off her long, slender legs, muscular from years of riding, leaned against the truck.

"Long day," she said, her loose hair blowing in the gentle night breeze.

He nodded.

"Are you hungry?"

Liam slipped his keys into his pocket with a nod.

"Callie made chili again. You seemed to really like it the last time."

"As a matter of fact, I loved it."

Kate tucked her hair behind her ear. "Join us for dinner?"

Liam sent her a tired smile. "That's the best offer I've had all week."

Chapter Four

"Man oh man." Liam sank onto one of the rocking chairs on the porch. "Your daughter is an amazing cook. I swear I haven't tasted any better."

Kate took the seat next to him, liking the feel of the hot mug of coffee in her hand, enjoying the night view of the land she loved. And, yes, having this new person in her life to talk about the events of the day. A person who seemed to appreciate her daughter in a way that she didn't often see. It didn't feel *normal* or *certain*, but it was a change. Perhaps a genuinely good one.

"She puts a lot of love into her food." She took that wonderful first sip from the hot, black coffee.

She caught Liam looking at her profile out of the corner of her eye as he said, "I believe that. You can taste when someone has put their heart into their cookin'."

It wasn't awkward, the frequent silences. Both of

them were exhausted from their busy days, and speaking seemed like a chore. After Liam finished his coffee, he sighed heavily, and she understood exactly what that meant. He still had a long drive and reports to write.

"Well…" he finally said, "I suppose it's time for me to hit the road."

Kate stood as well and held out her hand for his empty cup. She put the cups on a small table just outside the front door before walking with the veterinarian to his truck.

"I feel like I've had an awful lot to thank you for these last couple of weeks," she said, her eyes looking off into the distance.

They were standing closer than usual, Liam by his open driver's door and she facing him.

"I feel the same way." He reached out and tucked her hair behind her ear.

She looked at him then, drawn in by the kindness she saw in his bright blue eyes. "All we did was feed you a couple of times."

"No." Liam was slow to withdraw his hand as if he enjoyed touching her as much as she realized she liked being touched by him. "You've given me much more than just a couple of meals. I feel like I belong somewhere again."

He added with a laugh, "But don't give me wrong— the food matters too."

Kate felt a knot form in the pit of her stomach—was she ready to encourage Liam to feel like a part of the Triple K? It seemed too fast.

"Hey." Liam drew her back to the conversation, back to the present. "Go out with me."

Kate crossed her arms in front of her body, hunched

her shoulders forward protectively. "Won't that be a conflict of interest? You being my vet, me being your client?"

Liam, who usually laughed off things like that, didn't crack a smile. "Did you hire me just so you could keep me an arm's length away?"

"No." She laughed in a way that made it sound like a lie. "I hired you because you are a damn good vet, and I need a damn good vet."

For a second time, Liam seemed to want to jump several spaces on a game board. He put his hands on her face and kissed her. This time, it wasn't a peck. He took his time, explored her lips with his. And she let him. And she liked it.

Slowly, the most eligible bachelor in the greater Bozeman area lifted his lips from hers. But he didn't step away from her. His hands resting on either side of her neck, Liam waited until she was looking at him once again.

"I'll promise not to overcharge you, you promise to pay me on time. How's about that?"

"I always pay my bills on time," Kate said.

"And I never overcharge."

Any retort she was formulating in this oddly flirtatious banter was cut off by another kiss. Kate felt this kiss all over her body—little lightning bolts fired in her stomach, on her spine and between her legs. By the time Liam moved his head away, her head naturally followed.

When she opened her eyes, he was smiling at her, so fondly, and with a little humor.

"Where do you want to take me?" she asked him, knowing now that what they were feeling between them—this pull, this chemistry—wasn't something that she wanted to deny or ignore.

"Let me think on it." Liam gave her a final kiss on the lips. "I want it to be something real special for you."

"I think that's awesome." Lorrie had trailered one of her horses to the ranch for training. "You realized you've just bagged a man who has a high bounty on his head."

"I didn't *bag* him." Kate laughed. "He came willingly."

"That's the best way." Lorrie swung a Western saddle on her Appaloosa's back. "If I weren't already married, I'd have been all over that a long time ago."

That seemed to be the general consensus on Liam Brand. She knew that he was smart and handsome and successful, but she didn't know just *how* sought after he was. There were going to be a lot of sad bachelorettes if this "thing" with Liam worked out. Kate knew that the town was talking about them, and she didn't like it. What was there to be done about it?

"Hey, he likes you." Lorrie slipped a bitless bridle onto her horse's head. "They lost, you won. That's how the cookie crumbles."

Kate walked with her friend out to the nearby round pen where they would work for the next hour. Once Lorrie mounted and walked her horse into the pen, Kate followed and shut the gate behind them.

"It's not like this is a done deal," she told her friend. "We haven't even had one date."

"I've got a feeling about this." Lorrie told her. The woman was always having "feelings" about things—truth was, she was more often right than wrong.

Kate tightened the horse's girth before she patted the Appaloosa on the haunch. "Okay. Let's focus on training for now. We can start planning my wedding later."

It was an afternoon date, and Liam insisted that he pick her up at the ranch like a *real date*. They had talked on the phone every day since she had agreed to go out with him; they both agreed that going into town, the hotbed of gossip, wasn't the way they wanted to do it for their first date. Instead, Liam took her to his family's ranch, Sugar Creek, where there was enough room for them to ride up to the mountains on the property and have a private picnic.

It had always been difficult for Kate to be separated from Callie, but Fred, who had been the barn manager at Triple K for nearly twenty years, was the one person Kate trusted to watch Callie whenever she was away from the ranch. This was, however, the first time she had ever left Callie in Fred's care so she could steal away for an afternoon date with a hot veterinarian.

"I could have driven myself." Kate was still objecting to the fact that Liam had come to pick her up. It wasn't logical. "This is going to add hours of travel to your day."

Liam pulled onto Sugar Creek land: the Brands were a large family, wealthy, powerful and well-known. Liam had seven siblings total, and many of them had their own homesteads within the larger Sugar Creek holdings.

"This is my little corner of the world." Liam pulled up to a small log cabin.

"It's a really nice corner."

Once they were out of the truck, Liam gave her a

quick tour of his small homestead. There was a workshop with a shed, a four-stall barn and a chicken coop.

"I thought we'd ride up to the peak over there. I know
a spot that's got great views."

Her hands tucked in to the back pocket of her jeans,
Kate nodded with a smile. "Sounds perfect."

"I hope so," Liam told her. "I'm gonna grab our food
if you want to start tacking up. You'll be riding Doc
Holliday. You can't miss him. He's the big buckskin."

Kate found her ride and began to groom the beefy
golden quarter horse with hooves that looked like soup
plates and a beautiful black mane and tail.

"You're a good boy, aren't you?"

"He's one of the best horses I've ever had." Liam
walked into the barn with a soft-sided cooler.

"I appreciate you letting me ride him." Kate picked
up Doc's front leg to pick out his hoof before she made
the rounds to all of his hooves.

They finished tacking the horses, mounted and
started out on a trail that would lead them up to the
peak of the mountain off in the distance. It was a beautiful afternoon, sunny, blue skies, perfect for a horseback ride and a mountain picnic.

"Thank you!" Kate called to Liam, who had taken
the lead up as they entered the woods at the base of the
mountain.

Liam spun around in his saddle so he could smile at
her. "Having a good time?"

"Yes!"

Why had she fought this idea for so long? Why had
she deprived herself of the simple pleasure of spending a day with a man? It seemed reasonable at the time,

focusing all of her energy on the ranch and on raising Callie. But, now, it was beginning to be *her* time too.

They both loved to ride in quiet when they were in the woods; they had spoken about it more than once, and now that this was their first ride together, they honored that desire. It wasn't until Liam halted his horse at the end of the trail that they begin to talk to each other again.

"Sugar Creek is incredible, Liam." Kate dismounted and took the reins over Doc's head. "Your family is so blessed."

"God's country, for sure," he agreed. "But then again, so is the Triple K."

Yes, the Triple K was a beautiful swath of land—and she loved it and intended to live out her life there—but there was something magical about Sugar Creek. It was Montana beauty on steroids.

"We can leave the horses here. That way we can keep an eye on them while still taking in the view."

They tied off the horses, giving them their heads so they could nibble on some of the nearby foliage. Together, they climbed up the side of the expansive, gray, smooth granite that covered the top of the mountain.

"Oh, Liam!" Kate exclaimed as she got the full view the mountain provided. "I love it here!"

"I'm glad." Liam set the cooler down. "It's one of my favorite spots."

They sat down together on the sheer face of the mountain, side by side on a padded blanket Liam had packed for them. Her date had already interviewed her about her favorite foods, what she liked to drink and her favorite desserts. Yes, it was a private, quiet first date, but it was perfect for her. The effort he had taken to make sure he packed all of her favorites made her feel cared-for special.

"For you." Liam handed her a single, pink tea rose, her favorite flower.

Kate favored him with a small, pleased smile, as she took the rose, brought it to her nose and took in the sweet scent of the little flower.

He then handed her a wineglass.

"I can only have one of these." Kate watched her date pour her favorite white wine into the glass. "Drunk riding."

Liam laughed. "We'll be fine. I want you to stop worrying so much and start enjoying the day."

She raised her eyebrows at him in surprise. "Do I not seem like I'm enjoying myself?"

Liam rested one arm on a bent knee while he held out his glass to her so they could touch rims. "There's part of you that's not here with me. I'd like to have all of you here. Just for an hour or two."

After a sip of the wine, Kate tilted her head to the side and looked directly at Liam. "I'm sorry. I didn't know it was so obvious." She gestured to the side of her head. "My brain is always splitting duty."

"Hey…" Liam leaned on his side next to her. "I get it. It's hard to take a break. But just look at this, Kate. We're in paradise. Not everyone gets this gift. Wouldn't it be a crime not to give this 100 percent of our attention?"

"Actually. Yes. It would."

That was the turning point for Kate and her first date with Liam. She forced herself to put her stresses with the Triple K out of her mind, as well as putting aside her worries with Callie's future dreams and goals; instead, Kate focused her attention on the mind-blowing views that stretched for miles in the distance, and the handsome man who was bent on making her laugh and making her feel like a desirable woman again. The years had etched lines on her forehead, around her mouth and around her eyes. Those pesky nasolabial folds had deepened, and there was an annoying pad of fat gathering beneath her chin. It wasn't often that she dwelled over her aging appearance—she had a business to run and a daughter to support. But every once in a while, she would stare at her reflection and wonder where Kate King had gone. Liam wasn't the cure for all of that, yet his interest in her—the way he admired her face with his eyes—made her believe that she could still be a desirable woman. It wasn't too late for her.

Liam couldn't believe that he finally had Kate King on a date, on his mountain, after years of wanting to get to know her better. All of the pieces had just fallen into place for them, and at least physically, the horse trainer was sending off signals that she was enjoying his company as much as he was enjoying hers. They laughed together, they savored the silences together, and yes, they had a lot in common, starting with their passion for horses.

"Did you get enough?" Liam had already begun to pack up their trash and any food that hadn't been eaten.

"I did. Thank you."

He set the cooler aside, glad now to just look out over the land of Sugar Creek Ranch and beyond. Liam hooked his arms over his bent knees, turned his attention to Kate who was sitting cross-legged beside him on the blanket.

"I'm having a really good time with you," he told her.

"Me too." She tucked a few loose hairs behind her ear.

"You want to do it again?"

Kate turned her face toward him then; there was a softer look in her eyes now when she looked at him. Wordlessly, with the smallest of sweet smiles, she nodded.

"Good." He was satisfied. Getting Kate lined up for a second date before they had finished their first had been a part of his plan.

Liam lay flat on his back, sighed happily while he tried to figure out what shape the only cloud in the sky was forming.

"A sheep."

"What?"

"The cloud."

Kate tilted her head back, examined the cloud thoughtfully for a moment, then shook her head. "No. That's an alpaca."

"You're crazy."

She laughed and joined him. Kate leaned back, lay flat on her back beside him, her hands on her stomach.

"This is the most relaxed I have been in years, I think."

Liam admired her profile—he found that there were so many things for him to like about her. From her pixie ears to her strong chin and nose with the smallest of humps in the center. She was tanned from years of training horses outside, and there were sunspots on her shoulders and her chest. Kate was a salt-of-the-earth kind of woman—pretty in an unembellished outdoorsy kind of way.

"I'm glad." He decided to take a risk and reach for her hand. "You deserve to take some time for yourself, Kate."

When Kate King let him hold her hand, up there on top of his favorite mountain peak, Liam felt as if he had conquered the world. He didn't want to make too much of the date, but for him at least, this felt like the beginning of something rare, something unusual—something that had the potential to last for the rest of their lives.

They spent another hour up on that mountain, eyes closed, letting the cool air brush over their bodies, holding hands the entire time. The sun was slipping in the sky, and the temperature on the mountain had begun to drop. Kate hated to leave, she genuinely did, but it was time. As they reached Liam's small homestead, the sun was a bright orange ball disappearing behind the horizon.

"Thank you for the ride, Doc." Kate gave the large buckskin one last pat on the neck before she put him back in his stall with several pats of hay.

Liam gave her a quick tour of his modest bachelor cabin before she loaded into his truck. After she clicked her seat belt, Kate breathed in deeply and let out a long, slow, sigh.

"You okay?" Liam cranked the engine.

She nodded. "I feel happy."

After Liam pulled out onto the highway, he took her hand once again in his. When had she last held someone's hand like this? Holding hands had never really been her thing, but with Liam, it felt natural. It felt right.

"Callie was so excited that I was *finally* going out on a date."

"Is that right?" Liam smiled.

"Yes," Kate replied. "She thinks if I'm busy, she'll be able to do whatever she wants. Little does she know I can multitask."

She continued. "I never really hear you talk about your kids. How are they?"

Kate didn't have to be a psychologist to read the tension in the veterinarian's jaw and mouth—his children seemed to be a sore spot.

"They're great, as far as I can tell. We spend a lot of time video-chatting, but I sure as heck haven't felt like a parent for years."

She nodded, wanting to give him a chance to vent if he needed to.

"I don't feel like their dad, and that's the bottom line. Once my ex moved them out of the state, and remarried, I feel more like an afterthought than their father. This isn't how I imagined things."

"I'm sorry."

Liam's jaw jumped when he clenched his teeth. "No, I'm sorry. I don't need to end our first date by griping about my ex. My kids are great—I just miss them. And…it hurts to think about how much of their lives I'm missing."

Kate let the conversation about his children fade into talking about the new horse on his property. It was a nice neutral subject that they both could get excited about, and it immediately changed the mood in the truck from somber and tense to free-flowing with ideas.

"I'd actually love to bring Chief out here and have you work with us," Liam said, excited by the prospect.

"I'd love to work with you." Kate nodded. "I think he'd be a great prospect for a bitless bridle."

Liam pulled into her driveway, and Kate immediately began to think of all the things she had *not* gotten done by wiling the afternoon away with the handsome veterinarian. This was why she had such a hard time giving herself permission to have some downtime—all of her work backed up.

Liam hopped out of the truck and jogged around to her side so he could open the door for her.

"Thank you. Again," she said to him. "I had such a great time."

Liam was leaning back against the truck; he reached out, gently pulled her into his arms and kissed her. It was a sweet kiss, not too demanding.

"I have to go now." Kate took a small step back to break the contact. "There's always so much to do around here."

Liam walked with her up to her doorstep; he stayed at the bottom of the steps while she opened her front door.

"I'll be callin' you," he said with a tip of his cowboy hat.

Kate could hear that Callie was video-chatting in her room, which was the reason why she hadn't barreled outside the moment they pulled in.

"I'll look forward to it."

Chapter Five

As good as his word, Liam called every day. Sometimes she was too busy to talk; sometimes he was too busy to say more than "Hi, how ya doin'." But it was the fact that she had begun to count on that call that was the biggest surprise to her. She had to be self-sufficient, self-reliant, so it was really hard for her to relinquish any of the independence. Letting someone into her life felt as if she were giving up some of her independence, allowing herself to rely on another person, and that scared her.

"I-is Dr. B-Brand coming for dinner tonight?" Callie asked her as they, along with the other stable hands, finished dispensing the morning hay for the horses.

"As far as I know." Kate brushed loose pieces of hay off of her arms and shirt. "I asked and he said yes."

Callie had hay all over the front of her T-shirt; she

always hugged the hay to her body, no matter how many times Kate had showed her how to carry the hay in a manner that wouldn't result in covering her in loose hay.

"I-is he your b-boyfriend?"

Kate had been avoiding this daily posed question—Callie loved love, and wanted her mother to be in a relationship. Yet she still hesitated to label Liam.

The horse trainer handed her daughter a pitchfork. "I suppose so."

Callie took the pitchfork in one hand, but ducked her head and giggled behind her other. "Are you going to get married?"

Kate laughed at the thought. "No! We just started dating, Callie. That's too fast."

"Are you going to have a b-baby?"

Another laugh. "No, honey. I'm not going to have a baby. You're my baby."

"I—I'm not a b-baby." Callie shook her head, her face serious. "I-It's time for me to have my own b-baby."

Her daughter had been fixated on being a mother for years. Now that she had a boyfriend, that topic seemed to move to front and center all the time now. In addition to the obvious reasons why Callie shouldn't have children, there was the practical matter of basic knowledge about sex. Even after several sex education classes designed for individuals with intellectual disabilities, Callie still had a very naïve understanding about sex. For Callie, kissing was having sex.

Kate put her hand around her daughter's shoulders. It always hurt her to feel like she needed to regulate Callie's expectations for her future.

"We'll talk it about later, Callie. We've got a lot of work to get done today."

"There's always a lot of work to get done."

Callie was right about that. There was always something that needed to be fixed around the ranch. There was always someone getting sick or quitting or moving on—horses came and went, clients came and went—but she was always here at the Triple K.

"That's true." Kate nodded. "So, let's get to it."

Dissatisfied, Callie's smile dissolved into a frown. "When I—I marry Tony, I—I won't have to muck any more stalls."

"Let's cross that bridge when we get there, Callie."

The problem was, what was waiting for them on the other side of that bridge? It was easier for Kate to bury herself in the work, to focus on the business, in order to avoid this looming confrontation with her daughter. Callie wasn't letting go of the idea of moving to New York City and she certainly wasn't letting go of the idea of marrying Tony—this was a problem that needed to be addressed. Question was, what could she do to temper Callie's dreams with a shot of reality without crushing her spirit?

Liam headed to the Triple K after his last appointment. He'd been looking forward to spending the evening with Kate and Callie all day; the plan was to watch movies, pop popcorn and just hang out together. Having Kate in his life—a companion—was reviving all kinds of things in his life that were missing. Some he had known were missing, but other things, subtle things, were a surprise. It had been years since he'd made a night of popping popcorn and watching movies on TV, and it made him really feel like he had a family again. That was the type of thing a person did with a family.

"Hi." Kate, with her pretty, tanned face and pretty hazel eyes greeted him at the door.

He wanted to kiss her on the lips, but Callie was heading their way, and he wasn't sure if Kate would appreciate that. Instead, he kissed her cheek, lingering for an extra second to breath in the honeysuckle scent of her hair.

"Dr. B-Brand!" Callie greeted him enthusiastically, as she always did. "Are you hungry?"

He gave Kate's daughter a hug. "You better know it."

"I—I made franks and beans."

Kate shut the door while he followed Callie to the kitchen.

"That's one of my favorites."

Callie laughed behind her hand. "You say that about everything."

Kate hugged her daughter—Liam loved how affectionate they were—before she pulled a Mountain Dew out of the refrigerator, popped the top and then poured it into a glass without ice. Just how he liked it.

Liam guzzled the entire glass in several big gulps. He put the glass down with a smile. "I love Mountain Dew. It's not the best thing in the world to drink, but man, do I love it!"

Kate smiled at him, opened a second can, poured it into his glass and then pushed the refill toward him. The first couple of nights he had eaten dinner with them, she hadn't had Mountain Dew in the house. Now she kept it stocked for him.

After dinner, they all sat on the couch, with Kate sandwiched in the middle; on her lap was a giant bowl of popcorn, a little burned, and heavy on the butter.

"What's on?" Liam asked before he put a handful of popcorn into his mouth.

Simultaneously, Kate and Callie, leaning their heads together, said, "Hallmark Movies!"

Liam stopped chewing for a second, then finished chewing, swallowed and asked, "Are those action movies? Thrillers?"

Callie, her legs tucked up to her chest, rolled sideways toward her mother, laughing. "No! They're *romantic.*"

Kate smiled at him. "Chick flicks, back to back, all night long. Can you handle it?"

Liam made a face. "What do you take me for? An old-fashioned guy? I'm modern. I'm sensitive."

The veterinarian couldn't really care less about the movie—he cared about the company. He stretched out his legs, letting his thigh press up against Kate's thigh, and kept a steady stream of popcorn heading into his mouth.

In between bites, he pointed to the screen. "This is a Christmas movie."

"I know," Kate said in a dreamy voice. "It's Christmas in June!"

Callie leaned forward so she could see him. "Do you love Christmas?"

"Yes," he said truthfully. "I do. I like it in December, though."

"Shh." Kate hushed him. "You don't want to miss the beginning."

"Absolutely not," Liam said with a dead-pan expression.

Perhaps it was his full belly, or perhaps it was because he was just really comfortable in Kate's home, sitting on Kate's couch, next to Kate, but one minute he was watching a Christmas romance about a woman who unwittingly begins to date Santa's only son, and the next he was being awakened by Callie squealing in excitement.

"It's my b-boyfriend!" she announced loudly.

Kate's daughter jumped up and ran with her phone to her bedroom.

Liam sat up a little, rubbing his hand over his eyes. "Did I fall asleep?"

Kate was looking over her shoulder down the hall toward her daughter's bedroom.

"Yes," she said when she turned her attention back to him.

"Did I snore?"

"Yes!" She laughed. "I had to turn up the volume, it was so loud. You really need to get that checked."

"Man." Liam shook his head, embarrassed. "I'm sorry I fell asleep on you."

He put his arm around her shoulders and pulled her closer to him. He'd been wanting to sneak a kiss all night, and now that Callie was occupied with her own love life, it was his turn to focus on Kate's love life.

Liam hooked his finger beneath her chin and gently turned her face toward him. He kissed her, slowly, lightly, taking his cues from her. Kate didn't deepen the kiss; instead, she gave him one last quick kiss, and then moved her head away from him. He understood— she didn't want Callie to catch them kissing. Not just yet, anyway.

"I missed you today," he told her.

She didn't want to make out with her daughter down the hall, but Kate slipped her hand into his and threaded her fingers into his.

"Isn't that funny." She rested her head on his shoulder. "I missed you too."

They sat like that, in the silence, with the next Christmas movie in the lineup playing with the volume on mute, and the sound of Callie laughing and giggling drifting up the hall.

"Did she end up marrying the heir to the Santa Claus throne?"

Kate squeezed his hand with a little laugh. "Yes. As a matter of fact, she did."

He had begun to become part of the fabric of their lives. They expected him for dinner more nights than not, and Kate was beginning to count on his counsel. Liam was a levelheaded, thoughtful man. She tended to be black and white in her decision making—Kate also knew enough about herself to realize that she could make snap decisions that she would regret later.

"I know you have some valid disagreements with Callie's father," Liam said.

Kate raised her eyebrows and frowned. That was a serious understatement. Callie's father, Lloyd, had turned out to be a disappointment on every possible level, beginning with his outright rejection of Callie when she was born with Down syndrome. Yes, he had come around over time. But he was always letting Callie down, even as recently as last month, and he was behind in his child support by years. She had always been able to support herself, and her child, so Kate had decided long ago not to complicate her life by pursuing Lloyd for back child support.

"But he is Callie's father. And she wants to visit him."

They were sitting on garden swing beneath one of the old oak trees on the other side of the circle drive. It was a balmy night, humid and a little windy, with a promise of rain in the air.

Kate could hear in Liam's voice an echo of a man who felt as if he had been geographically cut out of his children's lives. But Lloyd was no Liam Brand. Liam was a dedicated provider who paid his child support; Liam was a man of honor and decency who treated Callie like a worthy and worthwhile person. Callie's father had turned out to be a major disappointment on just about every level a man could disappoint a woman.

"I know she does," Kate conceded. "She wants a lot of things. Not all of them are good for her."

Liam was quiet on that comment.

She breathed in deeply and let out a long, tired sigh. "She's never traveled without me. I have always been there, in the background, just in case. Callie has seizures."

"That I didn't know."

She nodded. "And the thought of her flying by herself, to New York…"

"Why don't you fly with her? You could catch a flight back the same day."

"I thought of that too," she answered. "But that's a lot of money. And time."

She sighed again with a shake of her head. "I love Callie more than anything. But she exhausts me."

"Hey…" Liam reached for her hand. "Let's just table

this for right now. You don't have to make a decision tonight."

Kate rested her head on Liam's shoulder. "I'm glad that I have you to hash this stuff out with. You know… I've never really had anyone to discuss Callie with before."

Liam pressed his lips to the top of her head, then rested his chin lightly on her hair. "I love being with you, Kate. I love being here with Callie and you."

She moved her head back, tilted her head upward, so he could kiss her lips. It didn't take any more than that silent invitation to bring Liam's lips to hers. He brought his hand to her cheek, deepened the kiss. That simple kiss lasted for several minutes, until Liam shifted uncomfortably and made a frustrated noise in the back of his throat.

He rested his forehead against hers. "Come to see me tomorrow, Kate."

She knew that there was more to that invitation than an afternoon of horseback riding. They had been in a kissing stage of their relationship for a while now—and it was sweet and lovely and tender—but their bodies were beginning to demand more. Much more.

In the low dusk light, Kate stared into Liam's deep blue eyes.

"Will you?" Liam rubbed his thumb over her lower lip.

She knew what she was saying yes to, and after another second of thought, Kate gave the slightest affirmative nod.

The horse trainer was rewarded for her response with another, deep, slow, passionate kiss from a man she was beginning to fall for, head right over heels.

* * *

The next day, Liam was waiting for her on his porch. When she shifted into Park, she noticed that he was pacing back and forth, his brow furrowed.

"What's wrong?" she asked him when he opened the door to her truck. "Are you okay?"

"I don't even know how to say this to you."

Kate had that sinking feeling that a person got when bad news was imminent. "Just say it."

Liam had almost a pained expression in his eyes; he looked around as if they weren't completely secluded. Instead of saying anything, he grabbed her hand and began to lead her into the house.

Off-kilter, and not expecting this greeting, Kate didn't resist being led into Liam's cabin, but pulled her hand from his.

"Tell me what's going on, Liam!"

He shut the door, his head bent for a moment, before he gestured to his groin. "I can't ride a horse like this."

Kate glanced down at his jeans and saw, quite plainly, that Liam was obviously aroused. As all women did wonder, she had wondered about Liam's endowment in that area. There was no need to wonder any longer.

Liam took a step toward her, his eyes so serious. "I've been thinking about making love to you, Kate. I *want* to make love to you. It's driving me just a little bit nuts."

She was temporarily stunned and didn't respond.

"I'm sorry," he added. "I know I was supposed to take you riding."

Kate finally laughed and threw her arms around him. "I thought you were going to break up with me!"

Liam took her shoulders in his hands so he could

look in her face. "Kate—don't you know that I'm crazy about you?"

Her heart gave a little jump of excitement as Liam wrapped her in his arms and pressed his lips to hers.

"Hmm." She loved the way this man kissed her.

A tingling began in that most private spot at the apex of her thighs; it had been such a long, long time since she had allowed herself to even entertain the idea of her own sexuality. She had been Callie's mom—her protector, her advocate—for so long, that she had abandoned her own needs as a woman. Liam was bringing all of those needs flooding back into her body with a vengeance.

Her hips naturally pressed into his and she wrapped her arms tightly around his body.

"Kate." He broke the kiss, his voice tense with desire. "Kate...?"

"I shaved my legs."

That broke the sexual tension, and Liam threw his head back and laughed. His eyes returned to hers as he brushed her hair over her shoulder.

"Oh, Kate. You make me laugh."

She was laughing too. She had no idea why in the world those words had come flying out of her mouth.

"Was that your way of saying 'yes' to making love?"

"Yes." Still laughing, she nodded. "Shaving my legs is a big deal. It doesn't happen all the time."

He took her to his bedroom and peeled back the clean sheets of his neatly made bed; then he peeled off her clothing before he removed his own. His body, long and lean, was a thing of beauty. Kate stared at him shyly from beneath the soft, cool cotton sheets. Was making love like riding a bike? Would her body remember what to do?

"You're beautiful, Kate." Liam joined her under the covers.

"You're handsome." Kate pressed the palm of her hand to his chest, taking comfort in the steady beating of his heart.

To the touch, Liam's skin was warm and surprisingly soft. Kate lightly scratched her fingernails through the brownish-blond hair on Liam's muscular chest. She hadn't ever considered herself to be a chest-hair fan, but on Liam, everything looked good to her.

Smiling at her with his eyes, Liam captured her hand, kissed her wrist. "We'll go slow."

"Not too slow." She moved closer to Liam.

With a satisfied groan, Liam pressed his body against her, his strong fingers roaming her back downward to the curve of her derriere. Their bodies pressed tightly together, Liam pulled the covers over their shoulders, cocooning them in their own private, sensual world. Kate dropped kisses down his neck and along his collarbone, her hesitant fingers exploring the contour of his back and shoulders.

"I am going to make you feel so good, my sweet Kate," Liam whispered into her ear.

His breath on her neck, the feel of his teeth gently nibbling on her earlobe, sent a shiver a pleasure down her spine. The center of her body ached for his touch.

Eyes closed, her head rolling back onto the pillow, Kate threaded her fingers through Liam's hair as he pulled her nipple into his mouth. Every touch, every kiss, felt like an awakening of something that had been dormant inside of her for years. Skin to skin, their legs intertwined, Kate sighed happily. Liam had been kissing her sweetly on the lips; at the sound of her sigh, he pulled away so he could smile down at her.

"It feels incredible to finally have you in my arms." He told her quietly.

"You feel good."

Liam's roaming hand slipped between her thighs; his warm hand cupped her, sending little shockwaves down her legs. Perhaps it was years of deprivation; or perhaps it was the fact that Liam was the sexiest man she'd ever known. But, when Liam began to play with her, rubbing her most sensitive nub with his finger, an orgasm, so unexpected and raw, crashed over her body. Her back arched, her arms wrapped tightly around her man, she pushed herself into Liam's hand. He stayed with her, pushing her to feel more, to keep riding the wave, until she was panting and languid in his arms. Liam kissed her eyelids, and her cheeks, and her neck, all the while murmuring sweet words in her ear.

Kate ducked her head into Liam's chest, embarrassed. It was so unusual to have a man want to give her pleasure without any expectation of receiving pleasure for himself. Liam held her close, gave her a moment to collect herself. When she was ready, Kate reached between their bodies and took him in her hand; quickly, the harness and the urgency returned to Liam's body.

"Do you have something?" Kate asked.

Liam leaned back, opened the nightstand drawer and grabbed a condom. He rolled away from her for a moment to put it on and then rolled back to her. The moment he covered her body with his, the moment he pressed himself between her thighs, Kate knew that this union was right for her. He filled her so completely, holding her hands above her head, while he rocked into her.

"Does that feel good?" Liam asked gruffly.

Kate wrapped her legs around his hips and held on for the beautiful ride he was giving her.

"Yes," she gasped. "Oh, yes."

He must have felt her tightening around him, must have known that she was building to another peak, because Liam quickened his pace, going deeper, pushing harder.

"Come on, baby," he urged. "I feel you."

Somehow, Liam knew all the right notes to play; somehow he knew all the right buttons to push. Twisting beneath him, Kate cried out again. This time, her orgasm was so intense, so strong, that Liam couldn't seem to hold back a second longer. Liam buried his face in her neck as he buried himself as deeply inside of her as he could. She felt him shudder and heard him groan; it was the most satisfying sound for her to hear.

"Are you okay?" Liam lifted up so he wasn't crushing her beneath his weight.

She nodded, afraid that she was feeling too emotional to speak. Making love to Liam…was unlike anything she had known before.

Liam left her for a moment to go to the bathroom; while he was gone, she curled onto her side, snuggled beneath his covers, and looked out the window at the mountains in the distance. She felt Liam climb into bed beside her; his arm went around waist and he pulled her backward into his body.

He kissed her shoulder. "I needed to do that. With you."

They hugged each other, quietly, until Kate heard

Liam begin to snore. She couldn't remember the last time she'd tried to take a nap in the afternoon and she wasn't so sure that she could. Instead, she lay beside her man, her mind trying to make sense of this new reality. They had taken a monumental step today; neither of them made love casually. This was, as much as anything, a commitment to each other and a commitment to their growing relationship.

Unable to sleep, and growing restless, Kate turned in Liam's arms so that she was facing him once again. Fast asleep, Liam didn't budge. Kate tapped her finger to the end of his nose.

"Liam."

"Hmm?"

"Are you awake?"

"Now I am."

She smiled. "I'm bored."

Liam stretched his arm in the air and opened his eyes; he looked at her groggily. "We can't have that."

He ran his hand down her arm. "What do you want to do? Go riding?"

"Yes."

"Okay. Let's go do that." Liam started to roll away from her, but she stopped him by putting her hand on his thigh. His eyebrow raised when her hand moved from his thigh to a more private spot.

"I didn't really mean that kind of riding," she said, knowing that her newfound brazenness was making her blush.

Willing, Liam lay back and let his woman have her way with him. Once Kate was ready to enjoy her creation, Liam rolled on another condom. Kate took him inside of her, sinking down until their bodies were joined.

"Hmm." Kate curled her body down onto Liam's chest, rocking her hips back and forth, her face breathing in the sexy scent of his skin.

Nothing—nothing—had felt this good to her. She wanted to savor all of the sensations she was feeling; the friction of their skin, the sensitivity of her nipples against the hair on his chest, the feel of his tongue in her mouth.

Liam held onto her bottom, pulling her downward so he could push more deeply inside of her. And, then, just like that, there is was again—that building, and pressure and sparks at the core of her body.

"There you go, baby," Liam murmured as she began to moan. "There you go."

Kate bit his shoulder, holding on to his body so tightly as she writhed on his rock hard erection. Her cry was stifled against his hot skin and Kate closed her eyes until the last shudders of the climax danced over her body.

After a moment to catch her breath, Kate sat upright with a surprised laugh.

With a tender smile, Liam said, "You're so beautiful, Kate."

Liam rolled her onto her back, rejoined their bodies so he could find his own release. And then the dance began again. He moved inside of her, hard, fast, demanding; skin to skin, legs intertwined, Liam thrust several times and then threw his head back with a growl of satisfaction.

"Lord, woman." Liam laughed, his forehead wet with perspiration. "I think you damn near wore me out."

Pinned down by his weight, their bodies slippery with sweat, Kate took his handsome face into her hands.

"You're the best thing that's happen to me in a long time, Liam."

Her lover kissed her sweetly on the lips. "My sweet Kate. I am yours for as long as you want me."

Chapter Six

"Thank you, Mommy!" Callie screamed while she simultaneously hugged her around the neck and jumped up and down. "Oh my gosh! Oh my gosh! I have to call Daddy right now!"

Was it the afternoon she had spent in Liam's arms, making love, talking, and then dozing off for a well-needed nap? Or was it just the fact that she realized that she was fighting a losing battle? Maybe it was a combination of both, but when she returned home later that afternoon, she gave Callie the greenlight to go visit her father and her sister in New York. It required her to block out two days when normally she would be training horses or clients, and it required her to spend the extra money, money that wasn't abundant, to fly to New York and back.

"I hope I don't regret this." Kate stared after her

daughter for a moment before she headed back into the barn to check on the progress of the evening chores.

As she always did, she swung by Visa's stall first. The poor boy, normally such an easygoing fellow, was beginning to develop some food aggression from being stuck in his stall for so long, pinning his ears and nipping at her when she brought him his hay. Liam was scheduled to x-ray the hind leg in a week; she was so hopeful that Visa would get the green light to go back to work.

"Fred!" Kate stood in the middle of the aisle, her hands on her hips, furious. "Where are you?"

Her barn manager came around the corner, a concerned look on his face.

"Yes, Ms. King?"

"None of these stalls have been cleaned." Kate pointed to several of the stalls. "This entire aisle is filthy. The water buckets haven't been washed today, and if I'm not mistaken, it's on the list for today, is it not? What's going on around here?"

"I don't know." Fred seemed as surprised as she was. "I'll get the crew on this right away."

"You do that," Kate said, annoyed. "These horses have a right to have clean stalls. They can't do it themselves."

Everyone who worked for her knew that she had zero tolerance for letting any of the housekeeping chores slide in the barn. She didn't have much of a temper, except when it came to slacking in the barn.

"I'm sorry, Visa." Kate rubbed the gelding's forehead. "We'll get your stall fixed up right away."

Now that she was taking some time for herself, all of the cracks that she normally filled when she was on-site were starting to show. She was going to have to rethink the business if she was going to continue to spend extra time away from the ranch. The thought of *not* spending alone time with Liam didn't seem like a good option. She had begun to count on that time for a little stress release.

Her phone began to ring; she pulled it out of her pocket, satisfied to see two stable hands enter the aisle with pitchforks and carts to begin mucking the stalls.

"Lloyd." That was the name that came up on the caller ID. It was a name she rarely saw, and she liked it that way.

"Hi, Lloyd."

"Katie."

Silence. That was how most of her conversations went with Callie's father.

"How have you been?"

Kate winced. Small talk with Lloyd was a less desirable task than getting her gums deep cleaned at the periodontist.

"Great," she said quickly. "I take it Callie told you the good news."

"Yeah. She just called."

Another odd silence. A sick feeling in her stomach, often associated with Lloyd, bubbled up in her gut. She moved down the aisle away from prying ears.

"Lloyd. What's wrong now?"

"Nothing." He sounded, as he typically did, like a worm trying to squirm off a hook. "Nothing at all really. It's just I didn't know about this trip, is all."

That information stopped her in her tracks.

"What do you mean, *you didn't know*?"

"I didn't know."

Kate took the phone away from her ear, closed her eyes, cursed under her breath several times.

What had possessed Callie to lie to her about something as big as this? Yes, her daughter was known to tell white lies, but this was a whopper.

"She told me that you invited her. That Bethany invited her."

"No." The sound of Lloyd scratching the stubble on his face, something he had done when they were together, made her cringe.

After another uncomfortable silence, she asked, "How did you leave it with Callie?"

"I told her that we'd work something out." Lloyd surprised her with that response, but with her ex, it was always "I'll believe it when I see it."

"You'd work something out? What does that mean? Is she coming to see you or not?"

"Well, now, Katie…"

"Kate."

"…this is all getting sprung on me out of the blue. I need to check my calendar, shuffle some things around—I'm in between jobs right now. You how my business is—feast or famine. Let's just see how it goes."

"Sure." Same old wait-and-see Lloyd. "Let's do that."

Without giving him the courtesy of a goodbye, Kate stabbed her finger on the red "hang up" button more times than needed to actually end the call.

"Damn him." She shoved her phone into her back pocket. "Damn him all to hell."

Kate went to find her daughter; she stood in the doorway of Callie's bedroom and watched her daughter balling up clothing and pushing it down into the open suitcase on her bed.

"Watcha doin', kiddo?" Kate walked over to the bed and sat down.

Callie had that smile on her face that she reserved for moments when she was super excited about something.

"I—I'm packing," Callie said happily.

Kate had to force down tears—tears of frustration and sadness for her daughter. Callie wanted to have a relationship with her father, and Lloyd had always let her down. No matter how gently or how often she had tried to explain the situation to her daughter, Callie simply couldn't grasp the complexity of the situation. In her mind, she had a father and he didn't love her. Maybe there was some truth to that simplistic assessment.

"Come here and sit down with me for a minute, okay?" Kate pushed the suitcase back a little and patted the mattress next to her.

Callie joined her and immediately leaned her body into hers and put her head on her shoulder. Kate put her arm around Callie's shoulders and hugged her.

"Sweetheart, I spoke to your father."

"Did he tell you that I—I was going to see him?"

"Here." Kate moved away from her daughter so she could look into her eyes. "Look at me."

Callie sat back, her brown eyes so full of hope.

Kate moved her daughter's long, brown hair over her shoulder before she took her hand and held on to it.

"Callie, your father told me that he didn't know about the trip."

Kate watched her daughter's face carefully. Callie didn't always know right from wrong, but she did know that it was wrong to lie.

Callie looked away, her cheeks and neck turning red and blotchy.

"Did you lie to me?"

Still keeping her eyes averted, Callie nodded.

"What have we said about lying, Calico?"

Her daughter slipped her gaze back to her for the briefest of moments. "I—I can't do it."

"Not that you can't do it—that you *shouldn't* do it."

Callie nodded again. "B-because it's wrong."

"That's right."

Her daughter's sweet face crumpled, then the tears began to fall.

"Come here." Kate took her daughter in her arms, just as she had when she was a little girl. She couldn't force Lloyd to be an engaged father; she could only be there, time and again, to pick up the pieces of Callie's broken heart.

"I—I wanted to go see my dad." Callie sniffled.

She wiped away the tears on her daughter's cheeks with her thumbs. "I know you did, sweet girl. But that's not an excuse to lie, Callie."

"I—I know. I—I'm sorry."

She stood, hands on hips, and assessed the mess in Callie's room. "How 'bout I help you clean all this up, and then we can go in to town and pick up some ingredients for whatever you want to cook today."

Yes, it was a temporary bandage for a wound that was never going to truly heal, but it was worth it to see a new smile on her daughter's face. This wouldn't be the last time that she had to deal with the fallout from Lloyd's absence in their daughter's life. That was just the harsh truth of the reality she had been living since the day Calico was born.

* * *

"It breaks my heart every time," Kate told Liam the next day. "Why does he have to be such a jerk? Yes, Callie did the wrong thing by lying, but she lied because she can't make sense of the fact that her father doesn't want to see her!"

"I don't know." Liam was sitting next to her in their favorite spot at the top of the mountain.

She glanced at his profile—they had agreed to keep talk about their exes at a minimum in order to focus on the present and their relationship. It wasn't difficult to read his unsmiling expression—her ex wasn't a top-priority topic for Liam.

"Sorry."

He reached for her hand. "You don't have to apologize. You need to be able to vent to me, and I need to be able to vent to you. We both have children with other people—no matter how hard we try, our past relationships will always resurface. I accept that."

She squeezed his hand gratefully.

"Are you sufficiently vented?"

With a laugh, she said, "Yes."

Liam had a real smile on his handsome face. "Good. Because I'd hate to think I schlepped this blanket up here for no reason at all."

She knew what he was driving at—one of her bucket list items was to make love outdoors, and today was the day they had slated to make love on their mountain. With all of her moaning and bellyaching, they were wasting time.

Kate stood quickly, stood in front of the man who had become more than just a lover—he had become her best friend—and pulled her T-shirt over her head and dropped it on the ground. Now she was standing on top of the mountain in her bra, the balmy breeze brushing over her naked shoulders and stomach.

Liam leaned back on his arm and took off his sunglasses so she could see his eyes admire her.

"You're a beautiful woman, Kate."

She smiled in response and unsnapped the button on her faded jeans. "Are you gonna keep talking? Or are we going to do this?"

Liam grinned at her, stood and pulled his T-shirt over his head. "Oh, we're definitely doing this, lady."

She had grown to love Liam's chest hair. She reached out and ran her fingers, tigress-like, through his light brown chest hair. Liam captured her hand and pulled her closer to him. He kissed her on the lips, on the neck, holding her tightly.

"Are we doing the full monty?" he asked against her neck.

She reached down between them, happy to discover that he was already aroused and ready for her.

With a laugh, Kate pushed away from him so she could finish undressing. "Yes. I want to be like Adam and Eve. Minus the fig leaves."

"You don't have to ask me twice." Liam winked at her as he stripped off his jeans and underwear.

He was naked, with the exception of his socks, before she could unzip her jeans.

"Something tells me that this isn't the first time you've been naked up here."

Kate unzipped her jeans, but she couldn't take her eyes off Liam. He was so well-built, slender, with lean muscle all over his body, tanned on his arms and neck.

The fact that he had a beautiful hard-on, just for her, only added to his appeal.

"Come here." Liam patted the spot next to him on the blanket.

Still in her underwear, bra and socks, Kate sat next to him on the blanket. He took her hand and kissed her shoulder.

"I like the way you smell," he said as he unhooked her bra.

"Manure and hay."

He laughed, gently slipping the strap of her bra down her shoulder. The moment the air hit her breasts, she knew that this feeling, this feeling of freedom, was exactly what she was looking to experience. She let him slip her bra completely off her body. Now sitting on top of their mountain, naked save her underwear and socks, Kate felt more free, and more adventurous, than she had in years.

As he always did, Liam began to fondle her breasts, massaging them just how he knew she liked it.

She dropped her head back. "Hmm. That feels so good."

"You feel good," Liam murmured before he kissed her nipple.

Kate thread her fingers through his hair, pressing his mouth harder to her breast. His mouth felt so good, so right. Her body was revving up, anticipating what was to come next. There was a tingling, an ache, between her thighs, building so quickly that she knew she would soon be pulling him on top of her, begging him to fill her.

"Lay back," Liam said, his eyes hooded with desire. She followed his direction, lifting her hips a bit as he slipped her underwear off her hips, along her thighs and past her ankles. Now she was naked, on a mountaintop, with the sun kissing her skin as the man she was growing to love kissed the inside of her thighs. She let her thighs fall open when Liam knelt between her legs. She knew what he wanted—he thought she tasted so sweet.

The moment his lips touched her, the moment his tongue slipped inside her, Kate forgot where she was and cried out with pleasure. With his hands beneath her bottom, Liam brought her closer to his mouth, loving her, tasting her, enjoying her. Kate moaned and writhed, pressing her head hard into her body; it was easy for her to ignore the sharp edge of the boulder pressing into her back. It was easy for her to lose herself and just enjoy the feel of Liam's mouth kissing her.

"You liked that," Liam said in a lover's voice as he kissed his way up her stomach and her breasts, until he was holding himself above her, the tip of his erection teasing her, asking for entry.

She reached for him with a pleased smile, wanting him so badly, needing him so badly. And then he was inside her, so deep, so thick. It felt like nothing else could. She opened her eyes and saw a look of sheer pleasure on Liam's face as he seated himself deep inside her.

"Oh, God, you feel good, baby."

The moment, which would have been perfect—which should have been perfect—wasn't perfect. The more Liam moved, the more the jagged edge of the boulder cut into her spine, and it hurt.

"Ow, ow! Wait! I have to shift," she told her lover.

Liam stopped moving, opened his eyes and smiled down at her. He braced his arms, lifted his hips off hers and gave her room to shift beneath him.

"Better?" he asked when she was done.

"I think so." She leaned back and lifted her hips to signal she wanted to continue.

They started the dance again, a rhythm they had developed over time. Their breath deepened, their eyes closed, and they both made noises of pleasure as they loved each other.

"Ow!" Kate's eyes flew open. "Wait!" She stopped moving. "Stupid rock. That really hurts!"

Making love on the mountain in her fantasy hadn't included sharp rocks poking into her butt and her back.

Liam laughed. "Hold on."

"Oh." Kate frowned as he disconnected their bodies. "It's not over, is it?"

"Hell, no." Liam lay down next to her. "You get on top. I'll handle the rocks."

With a smile, Kate put her hand on his stomach. "Are you sure?"

Liam checked the condom to make sure it was still secure. "Climb on."

She did climb aboard—happily. But then, her knees were rubbing against the boulder, ruining the pleasure of the moment. Frustrated and disappointed, her hands splayed across Liam's chest, Kate frowned. "This isn't working out as I imagined it."

"Don't worry. We'll make it work." She could tell, unlike her, he wasn't willing to call it quits.

Liam sat up a little, his arms braced behind him. "Here. Wrap your legs around me."

He positioned her so that she was sitting in his lap; it was the perfect solution. Now all she felt was his warm skin, his erection so deep inside her and the hard muscles of his thighs on her buttocks.

"How's that?"

She wrapped her arms around his shoulders, sunk her body down and began to move her hips. "Perfect."

She rode him, setting the pace, reveling in the feel of him suckling her nipple, reveling in the feel of his thick erection inside her. All she could hear was the wind rustling the leaves of the trees surrounding them and the sound of her moans of pleasure—and a laugh.

"Wait!" Kate whispered harshly, yanked back into reality. "Did you hear that?"

"No," he said against her breast. "Don't stop, Kate."

Another laugh.

They both froze their bodies, and looked around. "Is someone coming?"

"No." Liam tried to get back to business. "It's just an echo. They could be on the next mountain."

He tried to get her back in the mood, but all she could think about was getting caught, naked, doing the dirty. Liam was holding on to her, moving inside her. And, it felt so good, what he was doing, that he almost convinced her. Until she heard a male voice join that female laugh.

"Someone's coming!" she said urgently, separating her body from his. "Someone is *coming*!"

"Not me." Liam sighed in frustration. "Not any-more."

Chapter Seven

Kate was hiding behind a small clump of trees nearby, and Liam could hear her cursing under her breath as she yanked on her jeans and top. The moment, a moment he was *really* enjoying, was ruined. He had already pulled on his jeans and was bending over to retrieve his shirt when he saw his older brother, Bruce, the oldest of his six siblings, and Savannah, his sister-in-law, appear at the top of the mountain.

"Hey, brother!" Bruce, tall, broad shouldered, growing a beard, gave him a wave as he reached behind to make sure Savannah was safe.

Liam gave him a nod before he pulled on his shirt.

"Liam!" Savannah, as always, was happy to see him. She was a pretty, petite woman with auburn hair and moss green eyes.

"Who is it?" Kate asked harshly from behind the bush.

"My brother and his wife."

"Great," he heard his woman mutter. *Exactly. Great.*

Bruce and Savannah walked over to where he was standing, oblivious, at least in the beginning, about what they had just interrupted. Bruce clasped his hand and gave him a slap on the shoulder, and Savannah, now pregnant enough to begin showing, gave him a strong hug.

"We didn't expect to find anyone up here," Bruce said, looking around at the view.

Liam caught Savannah staring at the bra at his feet; for a brief moment, his sister-in-law met him eye-to-eye, her fair cheeks reddening.

"I think we should go." Savannah tugged on her husband's sleeve.

"Are you feeling okay?" His brother's immediate thought was about his wife's pregnancy. They had lost a son to a tragedy, and Bruce was hyperprotective of Savannah during this pregnancy.

Savannah, known for her sweetness, tried to smile through her embarrassment. "I just think that Liam wants to be alone…"

Bruce, who hadn't looked down and hadn't seen the bra, looked at his wife curiously, finding no particular reason why his brother would want them to leave.

"Oh, screw it," Liam heard Kate say from her hiding place.

Kate marched out from behind the shrubs, gave his brother and sister-in-law a little wave, scooped up her bra and tucked it into the front pocket of her jeans.

"Hi," Kate said with a little wave.

Understanding dawned on Bruce's face, but instead

of turning red like Savannah, he laughed a loud, hearty laugh and held out his hand to Kate.

"Nice to see you again, Kate."

"You remember my brother Bruce," Liam said causally.

Kate nodded.

"I'm not sure if you've ever met Savannah."

"Hi, Kate." Savannah shook Kate's hand. "We went to school together, but you were older, so…"

"I remember you. It's easy to remember the smartest student in school. Nice to see you again."

Savannah's face turned even redder at the compliment, one hand resting on her rounded belly, the other hand tucking a wayward hair behind her ear.

"I'm actually glad that we ran into you. I mean— I'm *not* glad that we interrupted what we…interrupted. Even though, it is kind of ironic because I was just talking to Bruce on the way up here that I needed him to text Liam so I could get your number. The whole family wants you to come to Sunday brunch."

Kate glanced at him—she knew that his family was aware that they were dating, but he'd deliberately shielded her from the craziness of his family's traditional Sunday brunch at Sugar Creek Ranch. His family was large and nosy and could overwhelm a person. He did not want Kate to feel overwhelmed while he was busy working his magic on her. Things were good between them, but by no means solidified.

"I think it may be a little soon for that." Liam blocked the invitation.

Savannah's expectant face turned crestfallen.

"Kate seems like she can handle herself," Bruce interjected. "Why don't you let her decide?"

Savannah reached over hand touched Kate's arm. "It's kind of like a rite of passage, but the food is amazing and everyone will love you. I promise."

"I can't leave my daughter alone and the person who watches her has Sundays off," Kate explained.

"She's welcome to come, of course!" Savannah assured.

Liam was surprised that Kate didn't seem completely opposed to breaking bread with his family. He'd eaten at her house dozens of times. Maybe it was the right time for her to run the gauntlet that was his family.

Liam ignored his brother and sister-in-law and turned to Kate. "I'd like you to be there. But only if you're ready."

Kate stared into his eyes as if she were trying to read his very soul before she said, "I think Callie would enjoy meeting new people."

His brother and Savannah left them to be alone on the top of the mountain after Kate agreed to join them for Sunday brunch. After their visitors were well out of earshot, Kate punched him in the arm.

"Ow!" He pulled his arm away jokingly as if she had really hurt him with that weak punch.

Kate held out her hand. "Underwear."

She knew that he had to have them because they weren't on the blanket where she had left them.

He shook his head with a smile. "No."

Hands on her hips, she frowned at him. "I'm not kidding, Liam! I can't believe that *this* is how I get introduced as your girlfriend to your brother and his wife! It's humiliating."

"No, it's not." Liam refused to give up her underwear and refused to give up on their mission to make love on top of this mountain. He'd never brought a woman to his special place; when Kate told him that she wanted to make love outside as a part of her bucket list, he knew that this was the right woman and the right place.

He pulled her into his arms even though she resisted half-heartedly. He kissed her on the neck, breathing in her familiar, sexy scent. God, he had actually fallen in love with this woman.

"They're gone," he said between kisses on her lips. "They won't come back."

"I'm not getting naked again if that's what you're thinking." Kate had her arms locked in front of her body, her forearms pressed against his chest.

"That's exactly what I'm thinking." He grabbed her bottom with both hands and pulled her groin into his. "Are you going to just leave me like this?"

"You're a big boy." She twisted out of his arms. "You can handle it."

He walked up behind her, wrapped her in his arms. He knew exactly what he needed to do to get her out of a "no" mentality and into a "yes" frame of mind. He began to kiss her ear, nibbling, licking, blowing and she immediately began to squirm in his arms, but not to get away.

She reached behind her body and put her hands over his erection. "You aren't playing fair."

"Make love to me, Kate," Liam whispered into her ear. "Right here. Right now."

She spun in her arms and kissed him, saying yes with her body, and her lips. Laughing, they stripped off their bottoms, but decided to at least leave their T-shirts on just in case.

"Crap!" he said when he realized he didn't have another condom with him.

"What?" Kate looked around expecting to see more people cresting over the mountain peak.

"I don't have another condom."

Her face went from relieved to thoughtful. "Oh."

They stared at each other for a moment, thinking. Then, Kate said, "I had my tubes tied."

That was news—they'd never really discussed it. They'd always used condoms.

He nodded, not upset. It was hard to think of either of them wanting to start all over again with a baby.

"We're...exclusive..." There was a question at the end of that statement.

"Yes," he said seriously. Definitively. "We are."

"I had myself tested after Callie's father. It's been a bit of dry spell since." she added with a raised eyebrow. "You?"

"I had myself tested last year," he told her. "So...are you okay with making love...without one?"

Her eyes drifted down to his softening hard-on, then back up to his face. "I am if you are."

Liam didn't bother to respond—he trusted Kate and if she trusted him, there were exclusive, and he wanted to make love to her in the worst way.

He lay on the blanket and she straddled him. They kissed and fondled and rubbed up against each other until he was good and hard and she was good and wet. Then, she sank on top of him, taking him inside her until he was buried so deep that it felt as if he were going to lose himself within her. She was so warm and tight and slick that he had to fight not to come right away. Without the condom, the sensations were so much more intense for him.

"God, baby." He gripped her hips with his hands, his eyes closed, fighting the feeling of wanting to explode.

"Is this okay?" she asked, her hands on his chest, her hips moving slow and steady.

"You feel so good, baby."

"I'm sorry." Kate stopped moving. "My knees. Can you sit up again like before?"

With one arm holding her close to his body, Liam leveraged himself into the sitting position. Kate wrapped her legs around his hips, and they were body to body, so close, holding each other so tightly.

Kate began to rock against him, taking her pleasure; this was a much better position because he could watch her beautiful face. He took her face in his hands and kissed her lips.

"Kate…" He said her name softly. "Open your eyes, Kate."

Her breath was shallow, her lips wet from his kissed. She opened her eyes. "I love you, Kate."

Her eyes widened in surprise at his words and, even though she didn't say the words in return, he could see the love in her eyes just before she closed them again; with a sigh, she wrapped her arms around his waist and rested her head on his shoulders. She came then, held so tightly in his arms, their groins pressed to together. She whimpered so sweetly, shuddering with the orgasm, Liam joined her. He had held off for so long that there was a sense of pain mingled with the pleasure.

"I love you too, Liam," Kate whispered.

Still connected, they held each other, their brows sweaty, their breathing rapid and shallow. For Liam, he couldn't remember ever feeling this way when he made love to a woman. This time was different—it was special. *Kate* was special. And it occurred to him, right then, that he wanted to make this woman his wife. He wanted to marry Kate King.

Kate was running late for Sunday brunch; he could tell by her harried voice on the phone that she was having "one of those mornings" when everything seemed to go wrong. Yes, things had gone wonky with her morning—a couple of hands called in sick and that put her behind. But he also knew that meeting anyone's family was stressful, and Kate had to be feeling that stress too. He knew he was, and to make matters worse, his father was on the warpath because one of his brother's daughters, a brother he hadn't spoken to in over twenty years, had been in contact with Savannah about her nonprofit. He'd almost told Kate to just scrap the brunch, but then again, she might as well see what kind of dysfunction she would be getting if she agreed to marry him.

"I don't give a good goddamn who contacted who and who did what first. I don't want any of Hank's kin on Sugar Creek Ranch! What in the hell were you thinkin', Bruce?" Jock Brand bellowed, slamming his hand on the table.

Savannah, whom Jock had always favored and had never had a harsh word for, spoke up. "I'm the one who answered Jordan on Facebook. Not Bruce. She wanted to donate to Sammy Smiles, and I wasn't going to turn her down. It's for Sammy's memory."

The table went temporarily quiet when Savannah mentioned her son, who had accidentally drowned when he was just a toddler. Savannah had started a nonprofit to spread the word about household hazards that could lead to accidental drownings, and everyone in the family knew that this was a "hands off" subject.

Jock frowned, his long, tanned, deeply lined face sullen. Savannah was pregnant on top of everything, and even Jock, who wasn't known for his sensitive nature, would be mindful of that. Instead of yelling at Savannah as he would any of his own natural born children, Jock balled up his fist, wrapped the table with his knuckles, pushed back his chair and left.

"I'm so sorry," Savannah apologized to the table. "We met Jordan's friend on our second honeymoon trip and one thing led to another..."

Bruce, ever protective of his wife, put his arm around his wife's shoulders and told her not to worry about it, as they all did.

After a moment, Lilly, his stepmother, a quiet, calm woman who had managed to last longer in marriage with Jock than any of them had bet, pushed back from the table.

"I will speak with my husband. Then we will have breakfast," Lilly said in a soft, but firm, voice.

"God—Dad is so uptight all the time." Jessie, the youngest, rather spoiled child and Jock's only blood daughter, was half paying attention to the discussion and half paying attention to her phone. "He really needs to seriously take a pill and get over it. Why can't I see my cousins? They didn't do anything to me, after all."

"Pop ain't gettin' over nothin'." Colten laughed between bites. "Pass those biscuits if no one's gonna eat 'em."

Liam looked at his phone to check the time—Kate and Callie were set to arrive in a few minutes, and he could hear Jock complaining loudly to Lilly about the breach of his long-standing rule—Hank and his kids were dead to them. Now, if any of them were communicating with their cousins on Facebook or any other social network, it would be mighty difficult to pretend that they were dead.

The doorbell rang and Liam got up quickly. He pointed his finger at all of his siblings. "Act normal. All of you."

"Ha!" Jessie laughed. "Fat chance of that!"

Liam beat Rosario, the house manager, to the door. "Thank you, Rosario. I've got it."

The woman gave him a curious look, then went about her business.

Liam swung open the heavy, carved door and greeted his love and her daughter.

"You have a b-beautiful house, Dr. B-Brand." Calico smiled at him.

"Thank you, Callie. Come on in."

He hugged Kate and gave her a quick peck on the lips. "Hi."

"Hi." She gave him a nervous smile. "Sorry we're late. Rough morning."

He shut the door. "Don't worry about it. It's been a rough one around here too. Let me apologize in advance for my family. They can be…challenging."

"Don't forget, I've already met everyone at least once." She was kind to try to reassure him.

"That's true," he agreed, leading to the dining room. "But you've never encountered them as a group. They can be a bit like a pack of wolves."

Kate, her hand holding on to her daughter's hand

tightly, continued to smile nervously. "We can handle them, can't we, Callie?"

"Of course," Callie said, confidently. "They aren't really wolves, Dr. B-Brand. They're just people."

Kate and Liam looked at Callie and then looked at each other. They both started to laugh; Callie had managed, in her own special way, to break the tension.

"I don't know, Callie," Liam said as he showed them to the dining room. "The jury is still out on that one."

Liam was damn proud of his family. They were on their "better" behavior for Kate and Callie, and they treated the young woman with kindness and acceptance and love. Lilly, who everyone called the "Jock Whisperer," had managed to get their hothead father back to the table. His face was still red and he looked as mad as a hornet, but his father had managed to be remotely cordial to Kate and Callie. That was more than he had expected.

"I can't remember the last time I ate so much food," Kate groaned as they walked the property surrounding his cabin. Callie had never met his horses or seen where he lived—it was time. While Callie visited with the horses for a bit longer, Liam took Kate to see one of his projects.

"Jock does everything to the extreme. He always has."

"That's not always a bad thing." Kate slipped her hand into his.

"No. Not always."

They walked in silence for a moment or two, heading to a large eight-bay garage. He pushed one of the bay doors open to show Kate what was housed inside.

"What's this?"

Liam smiled at the antique truck affectionately. "It's a Ford truck from the 1930s. It belonged to my great-great uncle."

"You're restoring it?" Kate, he could tell, appreciated the old truck.

He rested his hand on the rounded hood of the truck. This had been a project he'd been working on for years after he rescued it from the weeds.

"Little by little. It's a labor of love, really. One day, I'll take you for a ride in it."

On the other side of the hood, Kate smiled at him. "I'd really like that."

"So would I."

He was about to bring up the topic of a longer term commitment between them but was interrupted by Callie.

"Dr. B-Brand! I—I love your horses."

Callie, as she always did, greeted him with a hug.

"I—I want to b-bring my b-boyfriend here to meet them."

"That's fine," he told her. "Isn't it time you call me Liam?"

Callie ducked her head, blushed and then shook her head again.

"I told her she could call you Liam. She's just not ready."

Kate's daughter went to her side and hugged her. Then, she asked a surprising question to them both.

"I-if you guys get married, are we going to live here?"

His woman seemed caught off guard by the question—it made him wonder if she had even considered marriage between them. Yes, it was still early on in their relationship, but they weren't teenagers. They were old enough to know what they wanted and if something had a chance to work. Did Kate want more from their relationship? Or was he the only one swimming in that lake?

Kate brushed her daughter's hair over her shoulder. "We haven't talked about getting married yet, Callie."

Liam met Kate's eye. "Not yet."

That look held for a second longer, and then Kate added, "If and when that conversation does happen, you'll be the first to know."

Callie's giggled behind her hand. "B-but I—I saw Dr. B-Brand kiss you."

Kate wrinkled her brow at him over the hood of his antique truck—he had stolen a kiss, quite naturally, at the door earlier. It hadn't occurred to him that Callie had never seen them kiss, even if it was just a quick peck. He still had a lot to learn about Kate's daughter and how she saw the world through a slightly different lens.

"Yes." The horse trainer put her arm around her daughter's shoulder as they left the garage. "Liam did kiss me because we are really close friends. But just because you kiss someone doesn't mean that you are going to marry him."

"I—I am going to kiss Tony and I—I'm going to marry him," Callie said with certainty. "And I—I'm going to have a b-baby."

A pained expression flitted across Kate's pretty face. "Let's just take it one step at a time, okay, kiddo?"

Her mom's lack of enthusiasm, Liam noted, did not dampen Callie's excitement for the subject. "I-it could be a d-double wedding!"

Chapter Eight

Liam came over for dinner whenever he could—he was such a regular guest at their table that it was strange on the nights that he couldn't make it. And whenever she could, Kate took a couple of hours on his day off to meet him at Sugar Creek for a romantic rendezvous. There were plenty of bodies at the ranch to watch over Callie in the afternoon, so she had the freedom during the day to take a couple of hours just for herself.

"I hope you don't think that I'm just using you for your body." Kate had her body curled next to Liam's, her leg thrown over his, her fingers making circular patterns in his chest hair.

"I'm not sure I'd complain too much if you were," he admitted groggily, half-asleep after they had just made love. "But I'm glad you're not."

"Liam?"

"Hmm?"

"You're my best friend."

That was when he opened his eyes half-mast and looked down at her. He kissed her on the forehead and pulled her tighter into his body.

"You're my best friend too," he told her.

He dozed off, but she could never sleep in the afternoon. There was so much to do, all day, every day, that it was hard for her to shut her mind off even when she tried to sleep at night. The fact that she was willing to take an afternoon for herself was a huge change. After she untangled herself from Liam's body, she sat on the edge of the bed and stared at the man who had become her lover and her friend. He had kicked off the covers, and he lay on his back, completely naked, so handsome and strong.

Usually she would get dressed and kiss him goodbye. Today, she just couldn't resist taking control of the lovemaking for once. He was usually the one who initiated; he had mentioned, on occasion, that he wouldn't mind if she initiated every now and again. Perhaps it was time.

Quietly, slowly, Kate crawled over to where Liam was sleeping, glancing at his face to make sure he was still asleep. Gently, she took his penis in her hand, and, glad that he hadn't stirred yet, took him into her mouth.

She smiled when his body began to stir and his penis began to harden. Liam moaned, shifted his legs, and she felt his hand on her thigh.

Kate loved him with her mouth until he was as hard as a rock and ready to go, then she slid down on his thick shaft until their groins were pressed tightly together.

"Hello." Liam's eyes were open now, staring up her with a languid, sexy smile on his face.

"Hi, there," she said before she kissed him on the lips. "You don't mind do you?"

"Hell, no." He grabbed her hips and pushed her down hard as he was lifting up inside of her. "I love it."

At first the lovemaking was unhurried—she took her time building up to her first orgasm, and then she sighed as the sweet waves of pleasure pulsed through her body. Liam held her tight, letting her recover, before he rolled her onto her back and took charge. That's when the lovemaking became more intense, demanding; Liam grabbed the headboard behind her head so he could drive into her harder and deeper until she was sweaty and moaning and begging him to go faster. Liam exploded inside her when she started to cry out with a release so intense that it rocked her to her core. Nothing had ever felt like that before. No one had ever made her feel that *loved* before.

"What are you guys doing?" Kate had offered to wash the dishes while Callie and Liam spent some bonding time together.

"We're getting ready to video chat with Tony."

Kate sat on the couch armrest with her cup of coffee. "Is that so?"

Callie pushed the button on her tablet to call her boyfriend, Tony, and after a few rings, the young man who had captured her daughter's heart was on the screen.

"Hi, Tony!" Callie said with a giggle and a blush.

"Hi, Callie."

Tony was a little bit older than Callie, wore thick

glasses and had a crew cut. Callie thought he was the most handsome man she'd ever seen.

"Tony, this is Dr. B-Brand. My mom's b-boyfriend."

"Hi, Dr. Bwand." Tony waved.

"And you remember my mom, right?"

"Hi, Ms. King."

"Hi, Tony."

They gave Callie and her boyfriend some privacy while they went out to the swing under the old oak tree in the front yard.

"Are you okay?"

Kate didn't respond right away—her mind was racing, as it always did, whenever Callie spoke with Tony. Marriage was hard enough between two adults who didn't have a disability. You add Down syndrome, and marriage became nearly an impossible task.

"I just…" she started, and then stopped, not sure even where to begin. "Sometimes, I just don't know what to do with Callie. It would be different if there were other parents to talk to here, but there aren't."

"What about online support groups?"

"They're great. Don't get me wrong. But there's something different about face-to-face."

Liam didn't push her—he didn't rush her—he just waited for her to formulate her thoughts. This was one of the many things she truly loved about him.

"I know Callie hates it here."

"I don't think that's true."

"She does," Kate said with a shake of her head. "She wants to live in a city, where there are other people she can be friends with who have Down syndrome. When she goes to the yearly conference for Down syndrome, she's so happy. You should see her. She lights up. Here, it's as if the bloom has gone off the flower."

She breathed in and sighed heavily. She hadn't really opened up to anyone about her concerns regarding Callie.

"This is where my life is. I can't imagine living anywhere else, certainly not in a city back East."

"I didn't even know you were considering something like that."

She put her hand on his leg to reassure him. "I'm not. Not really. But what do I do about Callie? She doesn't have any friends here—she doesn't really have a life here. And she can't live alone. She'll never be able to live alone. She could live in a group home, but that would make me nuts. I would worry about her all of the time. *I've* been the one who's taken care of her since before she was even born. How can I just turn that responsibility over to strangers, no matter how competent and caring they appear to be?"

"I can't imagine you doing that."

"No. Neither can I. And now she wants to marry Tony and have babies. That's all she can talk about."

"And you don't want her to."

"It's not that I don't want her to get married and be happy, but it's so much more complicated with two people with Down syndrome. There's more than just Tony and Callie in this situation. Tony lives with his parents. Where would they live? Who would look after them? I haven't even really spent any time with Tony's parents. We actually have to get along and agree on logistics. Can you imagine that? There's more than just Tony and Callie in the marriage. Tony's parents are in the marriage too! Do you know what a mess that could turn out to be? Five people in a marriage instead of two."

"Is this…marriage even a possibility in the near future?"

Another sigh. She threw up her hands. "For Callie, it's a next week kind of thing. I don't know where Tony and his parents stand."

"Maybe it's time to talk to them."

She had been thinking the exact same thing, and then finding reasons every day not to call.

"I know. You're right. I've just been finding ways to avoid it. I don't know why."

"Because who wants to have that conversation? I'd find ways to avoid it too."

That made her laugh. She put her head on his shoulder, and they swung gently together in the night.

"You know what I'd like to do?" he asked her.

She shook her head.

"Take you out on a real, honest to goodness date. I always come over here, you come over to my place. When have we actually gone out?"

"I don't want to ask Fred to work an evening. He really needs his nights off."

Liam looked down at her, caught her eye. "Bring her along."

She lifted her head so she could get a good look at his face. "Are you serious?"

"She's a part of you," he told her. "Yes. Of course I'm serious. We'll all get dressed up and paint the town red. What do you say?"

"Yes." She kissed him on the cheek. "Of course, I say, yes."

* * *

She hadn't seen Baily, her master hairstylist and colorist for nearly a year. To sit in that chair, under those harsh lights, noticing every new wrinkle and facing sagging at the jowls, was rather painful. But if Liam wanted to take Callie and her out on the town, she needed to get her hair styled and get a new outfit. She spent her life in jeans and muck boots, smelling like manure and hay. Tonight, she was going to smell like perfume, with new hair and maybe even a dress.

"Are you going out on a hot date with Dr. Brand?" Baily asked while she combed out her wet hair.

It didn't surprise Kate that Baily knew about her relationship with Liam. It was a small town and the person who had managed to land a catch like Liam Brand was juicy gossip. But it still made her uncomfortable. She had been a private person all of her life, and even in a small town she wanted to have her business remain *her* business.

"He's taking Callie and me out to dinner, yes."

"Aww! That's so sweet!" the hairstylist exclaimed. "Handsome and nice to your kid? You need to get him to put a ring on it, quick."

Kate shifted in her chair, uncomfortable more with the topic of marriage than with her position in the seat. Liam had been bringing up the subject more frequently, and she just couldn't bring herself to get on board. Not that he was suggesting that they rush to marriage—he wasn't—but he did want to know if she had any intention of ever fully committing to him. For Liam, marriage and family had always been the goal. For her, marriage was never much of a priority. She had gone against her upbringing, her faith and her family when she decided not to marry Callie's father. His reaction to her diagnosis while their daughter was still in utero convinced her that Lloyd wasn't the type of man she wanted to marry. She was a businesswoman, independent and a single mother. Now she had an amazing man in her life as a companion and, in her mind, an incredible lover. Why rock the boat? Marriage could, ultimately, destabilize a really good thing that they had going.

"Look, Mommy!"

Callie had been in the front of the salon getting treated to a manicure and pedicure in preparation for their big night out with Liam.

She extended both of her arms and wiggled her bright pink fingernails for her mother to see.

"Pretty in pink!" Callie told her.

Kate leaned over and kissed her daughter's happily flushed cheeks. "You are pretty in pink, kiddo."

"Thank you." Her daughter ducked her head. "I—I need to take a selfie for Tony so he can see how pretty my nails are."

"I'll take a picture of you," Baily offered.

Baily took a break from her duties with Kate's hair to take a picture of Callie with her hot pink nails. Then, Callie sat in the empty chair next to Baily's station and focused on her phone.

"She's so grown up," Baily commented as she picked up her scissors. "I can't hardly believe it."

"I know." Kate nodded. "It's seems like yesterday I brought her in for her first haircut."

"Time flies, don't it?"

"Yes, it does."

Baily stood behind Kate and met her eyes in the mirror. "So. How much are we taking off?"

Kate stared at her own reflection, finding it difficult to focus on anything other than how haggard and old she was looking to her own eyes. After a moment of thought, she shrugged. "It's time for a change. As long as I can get it into a ponytail, I'm good."

Baily held a chunk of hair between her fingers and held it up for Kate to see. "Three inches would make a world of difference."

It had been years since her hair had been that short. And, yet, things were changing all around her and it felt like that should be reflected in her hair.

"Go for it," she said. "If I don't like it, I can always grow it back."

"Wow." Liam stared at her as if he were seeing her for the very first time.

"It's a lot shorter than I thought it would be." Kate self-consciously touched her bobbed hair.

"You look…" Liam's eyes continued to admire her. "You look so beautiful tonight, Kate."

She hadn't worn a dress since Callie's high-school graduation the year before. Tonight, she wore a simple green wrap dress and a simple pair of strappy heels. Green was Liam's favorite color; she had wanted to look especially nice for him tonight.

"Thank you. You look handsome."

Liam was wearing a sport coat, a crisp white shirt and dark denim jeans. So handsome, this man of hers.

"Hi, Dr. Brand!"

"Calico! Look at you."

The young woman held out her hands and wiggled her fingers. "Pretty in pink."

Liam took one of her hands, kissed it and then spun her around. "You look beautiful."

Callie covered her face with her hand and giggled with pleasure. Liam offered each one of them his arm.

"Shall we?"

As they drove into town in Liam's freshly cleaned truck, listening to strains of Trace Adkins, all Kate could think about was how kind Liam was to her daughter. Why hadn't Callie's own father been able to be even half as kind?

"You okay?"

Kate pulled herself away from her thoughts of Callie's father and gave her companion a quick nod meant to reassure.

"I've been looking forward to this all day," she said, because it was the truth.

He took his hand off the steering wheel for a moment to squeeze her hand. "So have I."

From the back seat, Callie chimed in. "I—I have too!"

Liam took them to Emerson Grill, known for its fine Northern Italian cuisine. Callie had a very limited palate, so she stuck with spaghetti marinara and meatballs. To drink, a Shirley Temple from the bar. Yes, Kate loved spending the evening with Liam and her daughter. More than that, she loved to see how happy her daughter was to be dressed up, with her nails polished, "out on a date." It made Kate wonder—was she being selfish keeping Callie in Montana with her? Was it time to let her go?

After dinner, they caught a PG movie, and then Liam drove them home. The first thing Callie did was get on her tablet to video chat with Tony. Kate slipped off her shoes, dropped them on the floor and then joined Liam on the couch. She leaned into his body, her back resting against his chest, her head tilted to the side so it was tucked into the crook of his neck. She loved the way this man felt; she loved the smell of his skin and the feel of his hands on her body.

"Hmm," she murmured, her eyes closed. "This is nice."

"You feel nice."

His voice was groggy, and she knew him well enough to know that if she just stopped talking to him, he'd be asleep in no time. Liam had never spent the night at her house, not even on the couch. The man was so tired, it just didn't make sense for him to drive the hour it would take him to get back home.

Kate slowly extracted herself from Liam's arms, helped him out of his boots and then covered him with the blanket that she kept draped over the back of the couch. She kissed him on the cheek.

"Thank you for tonight, Liam."

He mumbled, eyes still closed, "I love you."

It was so easy for him to say to her, and yet, those words always seemed to get stuck in her mouth right before she got them out. She did love Liam—and she had managed to tell him once before. Honestly, loving him was a no-brainer. He was kind, and smart, and successful, and funny. He was so good with Callie. Why couldn't she commit herself completely to this man? Was she permanently broken? Or just too set in her ways to imagine her life as a plus one.

After she gave Liam another kiss good-night and checked on Callie, Kate went to her bedroom, got ready for bed and turned off the light. Normally, she was so tired that pretty much the second her head hit the pillow she was asleep. Tonight, she stared up at the ceiling, her mind whirling. She tossed, turned and then finally snapped on the light and threw back the covers. Sitting on the edge of the bed, beyond irritated to still be awake when she was tired as heck, Kate finally got up.

Long after Liam and Callie had gone to sleep, Kate sat up paying bills and answering emails. She just couldn't seem to get her brain to shut off, so she figured she may as well get some work done. Several hours later, she stood, stretched, her neck stiff and back aching.

"Okay," Kate said aloud to herself. "Let's try this again."

Once again in bed, Kate lay on her back, her arms under the covers, eyes wide open. And the truth was, she knew what was keeping her awake. This was the first time a man had spent the night in her home, and it was freaking her out. All he was doing was sleeping on her couch. He hadn't asked her to marry him, even though he had hinted at it, and he hadn't moved his stuff into her drawers. And, yet, this felt like a giant step further into relationship-land.

"Kate Marie." She blew out her breath. "It's not the end of the world, it's just the next natural step. What's *wrong* with you?"

Chapter Nine

"**I**'m exhausted." Her friend Lorrie hoisted her saddle onto the rack and slumped down onto her tack trunk.

Kate continued to clean the bridle she had just used on the trail ride she had taken with her friend.

"Everyone in the house has been sick except me." Her friend leaned back and closed her eyes. "I think this may be the first time I've closed my eyes in days."

The horse trainer finished her chore, hung up the bridle and then said, "Let's go get something to drink before you head out. I feel like it's been forever since we've had a chance to catch up."

"It's been a while." Her friend sighed before she opened her eyes. "You've been busy, I've been busy."

Lorrie dropped her hands on her thighs with another sigh, groaned a bit from the sore leg muscles when she stood. "I've been feeling so guilty about not coming out here and riding."

Side by side, they walked out of the barn, stopping to give some love to the old cats gathered at the entrance of the barn. They took the stairs up to Kate's office above the barn, where a pot of coffee was ready to brew.

Her friend sat on the small love seat. "That coffee smells so good."

"It'll be done in a second." Kate sat, kicked her boots off and put her feet up on the desk.

"So…" Lorrie eyed her with interest. "How's it been going with the hot veterinarian?"

"It's going fine." She shrugged noncommittally. "So far."

A disappointed expression passed over her friend's face. "Oh."

The bubbling, popping sound of the coffee at the tail end of brewing got Kate out of her seat. "What?"

Lorrie wrinkled her nose a bit. "Is the sex bad?"

Kate kept on pouring coffee into a cup as she gave a surprised laugh. "Why would you think that?"

She handed her friend a cup and sat back down one of her own.

"Because…" Lorrie blew on the coffee. "If it was good, you wouldn't use such a horrible word like *fine* to describe your relationship."

Lorrie took her first sip of coffee. "Ah. Thank you. This is exactly what I need to help me make the drive home."

"Fine just means fine. As in, everything's fine between us."

"Fine," Lorrie said with a teasing laugh.

That made Kate smile into the rim of her cup. The

coffee did taste good, and it would give her the pick-me-up she needed to help her get the rest of the work on her daily to-do list done.

"No…" She put her cup on the desk. "Liam is more than fine. He's so kind. Considerate. A real adult, which can be really hard to find in a man…"

"Amen."

"…and he is so amazing with Callie. He treats her like she matters. He always has. I only wish I could have gotten Lloyd to treat her with half as much love and care. All he's done is disappoint her. Remember I told you about the phone call and Callie packing?"

Lorrie nodded.

"Well, I called yesterday, no answer. I called the day before. No answer. I've texted, emailed."

"No answer." Her friend filled in the obvious response.

"He's such a jerk," Kate said with a frown. "Callie deserves so much better."

"She has better now."

Kate looked up.

"Liam," Lorrie told her. "She has Liam."

"That's true," she agreed. "But nothing is set in stone there. And I'm still not sure where it's going yet."

"Do you want it to go somewhere?"

Lorrie knew her like no other, and her friend had managed to ask *the* question. Where did she want things with Liam to go?

Her friend got up to refill her cup; she held up the coffeepot. "More?"

Kate put her hand over the top of her cup with a shake of her head.

With a refreshed cup of coffee, Lorrie took one of the armchairs on the other side of Kate's desk.

"Do you think that you would ever get married?" her friend asked. "If the right man—like Liam—came along?"

She crossed her arms in front of her body.

Lorrie filled in the silence. "It's hard to give up control, I would think. You've been the head of your own life for years."

"I try to imagine what it would be like to have to answer to someone else. I'm not sure I'm really cut from that cloth."

"Liam seems like he's cut from that cloth."

Yes. Liam was definitely the marrying kind.

"We haven't talked about it, really. Not in so many words. He's hinted and I've avoided."

With a sigh, the horse trainer stood. Break time had to be over. "Why does every relationship have to end in marriage? I *like* how things are between us. He has his space, I have mine. We see each other when our schedules allow. What's wrong with that?"

"Nothing at all. It's not written anywhere that you have to get married, Kate." Lorrie stood up as well, rinsed her mug out in the sink. "Liam and you can go on like this forever, if that's what you both want. Is that what you both want?"

"Well?" Kate asked, a hint of anxiety in her voice. "Can he go back to work?"

Liam had his computer set up on a small folding table, examining the X-rays he had just taken of Visa's hairline fracture.

Visa had been a worry in the back of Kate's mind;

Liam had already been out once before, and the fracture hadn't healed enough for him to "okay" a return to work.

Liam looked up from the radiographs. "He can go back to work."

Kate's face lit up in a way that pleased him. He'd grown to love the planes of her face, the sweetness in her eyes, and the taste of her lips. He missed her when they were apart, and he couldn't wait to get her back in his arms the moment he saw her.

"Did you hear that, Visa?" Kate unhooked the straps for the cross ties and led the horse out of the bay. "You just got released from jail."

Liam walked beside Kate and Visa as she led him past the stall that had been his cell for the last several months. He had something to talk about with Kate, and he hoped that she would be as excited as he was about the news.

Kate took off Visa's halter and released him to a small fenced pasture where he could get the "silly" out, running and bucking and rolling on the ground without any interference from other horses.

The minute Visa realized that he was free, he began to run from one end of the small pasture to the other, kicking and bucking happily along the way.

One of his interests as a large-animal veterinarian was helping to heal and return to full function horses that would otherwise be put down because of an injury.

Kate, surprising him, wrapped her arms around his waist and squeezed him tightly. She didn't say anything, but she didn't need to. Her animals, all of them, were second only to Callie. Saving Visa, such a young, beautiful horse with so much life left to live, was a gift to her. And she appreciated him for it.

Liam held on to the woman he loved, his chin resting lightly on the top of her head, loving the smell of the honeysuckle shampoo that she used.

"I really thought I was going to lose him," she said after a moment.

"I was going to do everything in my power to make sure you didn't."

She unwound her arms from his waist, and he reluctantly let her go. Kate was affectionate only to a point, and rarely in public. And he understood. Here at the Triple K she had to maintain a strong leadership image for the men under her charge. Even in the new millennium, there was a lot of sexism in the industry. It couldn't always be easy to be the boss of men.

"You are one hell of a good vet, Liam." She leaned forward, resting her arms on the top of the fence. "I'm grateful to have you."

"Thank you." Liam joined her at the fence. "I'm glad to be here for you."

He wanted to be there for Kate in all aspects of her life—not just as her vet, not just as her part-time lover and boyfriend. He wanted more. But he also knew, just from her body language and facial expressions and avoidance, that trying to move their relationship further along would only be met with resistance. It was early enough in the relationship that he could afford to be patient. Yet if Kate wanted the status quo to go on indefinitely, that wasn't what would work for him. He craved companionship; he craved family. He wanted Kate and Callie to be his family.

They left Visa to graze happily in the pasture. Liam

had seen him trot and gallop without any sign of lameness. Visa was one of his best success stories, and particularly because he was one of Kate's horses, he was gratified that his plan for the young gelding had worked. There had been no guarantee that it would.

"Can you stay for dinner?" she asked as they walked through the barn back to his equipment.

"Not tonight." Liam began to pack up his gear.

It satisfied his ego to see a flash of disappointment in her eyes. It felt good to know that she wanted him to be with her, even if he couldn't be there as much as he wanted to.

Liam lifted his gear, and they walked out to his truck together. After he loaded his equipment, Liam stood next to the open driver's door.

"Callie's going to be disappointed you can't make dinner." Kate squinted against the sun.

"How about her mom?"

"She'll be disappointed too."

"Good," he said with a smile. "That's exactly how I want it."

He snuck a quick kiss before he said, "Today is a good news day all around."

She waited for him to continue.

"My kids are coming for a visit next week."

Kate's face lit up. "Liam! That's great news. I'm so happy for you."

He climbed behind the wheel. "I want them to meet you."

"Of course."

"And Callie."

Kate nodded without any hesitation in her eyes.

Liam shut the door, cranked the engine, then hung his arm out of the window. "I'll talk to you tonight."

She nodded again with a wave. They had begun a ritual of speaking on the phone every night before they went to bed.

"Hey." He started to pull away, then stopped. "I love you."

He was rewarded with a fleeting, sweet smile. "Me, too."

"Good," he said again. "That's exactly how I want it."

His kids looked different in real life—he'd been communicating with them via phone, video chat, email and text, everything but face-to-face for so long that it seemed strange to have them in the truck with him again. They were taller, older, different.

"You guys hungry?" Liam had just picked up the two teens from the airport.

"I'm gluten-free." Sarah didn't look up from her phone.

"Since when?" he asked his younger child, who had begun to mature into something resembling a woman now. She was wearing lip gloss.

"Since forever," his daughter said rather sullenly. He was well aware of the fact that Sarah hated her new school, hated her stepfather, hated Seattle, and, in general, currently hated her mother.

"Well, don't worry. I'm sure we can find some gluten-free food for you. I won't let you starve."

"Sure you won't." When had Sarah become so sarcastic.

"What about you?" he asked his son, also engrossed in his cell phone.

Both of his kids, like so many other kids nowadays, were total phone junkies.

"I could eat," Cole mumbled.

"Mom wanted me to tell you that Cole has to watch what he eats because of he just got his braces."

"Mind your own business," Cole snapped at his sister.

Sarah kicked under the passenger seat in response.

"Your daughter can be a real asshole."

Yes, he'd expected them to be different, but these were completely changed kids.

"Watch your language, Cole."

"Ooh. You're in trouble now, jerk."

Liam caught his daughter's eye in the rearview mirror. "What the heck is wrong with the two of you? You guys actually used to like each other."

It was a tense, quiet lunch, with Sarah complaining mostly about the lack of gluten-free selection. They stopped at the grocery store to pick up gluten-free food for his daughter and stock up on some snacks for his son. Cole spent most of the trip laughing at something his friends put on Snapchat while Sarah took charge of the shopping cart. He had his kids back with him for not even a half a day, and already he wanted to send them back. And he felt like a horrible person because of it.

"Everything in your rooms is the same," Liam told them when they got back to the cabin he had built as a wedding gift for their mother.

When they arrived at the ranch, a place they had called home for the first part of their lives, that was the first time he actually saw some lightness, some happiness, come into his daughter's blue eyes. It had been fleeting, but it had been there. That was a start.

Cole went straight into his room and shut the door.

"Great." Sarah paused in the doorway. "My Little Pony."

Liam stood in the great room staring at the two closed bedroom doors. This was not how he had imagined his first day with his kids. He'd look forward to this for such a long time, and it was off to a dubious start at best.

"So? How's it going?" Kate picked up her cell after the first ring.

He had stepped outside and walked over to his workshop, away from the house so his kids couldn't hear his conversation.

"Honestly." He shut the door to his workshop behind him. "They act like I'm punishing them by even having them here."

"Oh," Kate said sympathetically. "They're teenagers. It's their job to act like everything is a pain in their neck. Just give them a couple of days to shake off the grumpiness, and I'll bet they'll warm up."

He hoped she was right. One week of sullen and sarcastic would be a long week indeed.

"I think we should postpone our dinner with them."

"Sure," she said easily. "Let's just keep it flexible. There's always next time."

"No," Liam said quickly. "I want them to meet you and Callie this time. I'll talk to you tonight."

The week had passed quickly for her, but it was strange not to have Liam around. His children's visit was keeping him occupied, and the only time they really had a chance to talk was at night. She missed him. She missed making love too. Her body was actually letting her know that it missed having private time with Liam.

He met her and Callie at the door of his cabin.

"Hey!" He didn't kiss her as he usually did, but the smile on his face and the smile in his eyes let her know that he was as glad to see her as she was to see him.

"Hi, Dr. B-Brand. I—I made a gluten-free chocolate cake for you."

"Thank you, Callie." Liam gave her a hug and accepted the cake. "This looks so good I may have to have dessert first."

That made Callie duck her head with pleasure and giggle.

Liam introduced him to his teenagers. Both of his kids strongly favored Liam and the Brand side of the family; both were tall, lanky, with sandy-brown hair and bright, blue eyes. Sarah, in particular, was the spitting image of her father.

"Have you been enjoying your visit with your dad?" Kate tried to make a connection with Liam's daughter.

Sarah shrugged a little. "I used to live here."

"I remember," the horse trainer told her. "I used to see you in town with your mom."

"Yeah."

"Do you miss it?"

Sarah shrugged again.

"Do you like horses?"

That got the smallest of smiles out of the teen.

"I used to ride all the time when I lived here," Sarah told her. "I never get to ride in Seattle."

"You can come out to see my horses if you want," Kate offered.

"We have horses here." The teen pulled a face.

Sarah stood, looked as if she was going to leave without say anything in response, but she stopped and said, "Dad didn't tell me he was dating anyone."

Every second his kids were with Kate and Callie, Liam felt like he was on edge. He didn't relax from the time Kate had arrived until the time he was walking them out to their truck. They both waited for Callie to get inside the vehicle before they took a moment to talk privately.

"I'm sorry." Liam apologized right off the bat, even though she didn't expect it or think it was warranted. "They're going through a weird phase. God help me if they get stuck in it."

Kate touched his arm sympathetically. "A week is such a short time. Couldn't they stay a little while longer?"

"Perish the thought," Liam blurted out before he added. "No. Their mother and stepfather are taking them to the Bahamas."

"Well, I'm glad I got to meet them, anyway." She had seen Liam's children at school functions in passing, but that had been years ago. They had both grown so much since then.

Liam looked pained; none of this was easy for him. He wanted his kids to love their time with him, and he wanted them to love her too.

"It's going to be okay, Liam. It always is."

Chapter Ten

"Lord have mercy, I needed that." Kate rolled onto her back, naked.

Liam chuckled, his hand on her thigh. "I second that."

After taking a week off to spend with his kids, Liam had to work late nights without taking a day off to catch up with his caseload. No day off meant no time for afternoon lovemaking.

Kate pulled the covers over her body and curled into Liam's warm body, loving the scent of the man. She kissed his chest, before resting her head in the crook of his arm.

"I can't believe how much my body missed you."

Liam lifted his head a little to look down at her. "Just your body?"

She hugged him. "No."

"I missed you," he told her, rubbing her arm lightly. "I miss you all the time."

"Hmm…that's nice."

Liam sat up so he could look down at her; he brushed her hair away from her face.

"Every night that we talk on the phone, I say sweet dreams before we say goodbye and then I wonder why I'm not with you, in person, to kiss you good-night."

She reached up and put her hand on his face. "We live complicated lives."

"Not really," he disagreed gently. "It doesn't have to be complicated. Why can't we live together? I love you, I love Callie. As far as I can see, there's nothing holding us back."

Kate tried to scoot away from him, but Liam rolled between her thighs and pinned her down.

"Every time I try to talk to you about our future, you find a reason to end the call or change the subject or find something, anything, else to do."

He kissed her before she could formulate words; she'd rather kiss him than talk about taking the next step in their relationship when she wasn't all that sure that they *needed to* take a next step. This was lovely.

Kate let her legs fall open wider, wrapped her arms around Liam's waist; she felt his body begin to rouse and she welcomed the diversion. Liam reached between their bodies and guided his hardening shaft into her body.

"Ah…" Kate sighed at the wonderful feeling. Slowly, deliberately, Liam pushed into her deep, then stopped moving. They were connected, body to body, chest to chest.

"Look at me, Kate."

Liam had lifted himself up over her.

She opened her eyes; he had grown so hard so quickly that she wanted to stop talking and start moving. It was so easy to orgasm with Liam.

"This is incredible." Liam's voice was gruff with feeling, desire. "But there has to be more."

Kate nodded and shifted beneath him to get him to move within her. It took only two long, hard strokes to get her to climax. She shuddered in his arms, clinging to him, wrapping her legs so tightly around him as he picked up the rhythm, driving into her until he found his own release.

Instead of lingering in bed with her as was his habit, Liam gave her a quick peck on the lips, got out of bed and hopped into the shower. She wasn't stupid—her resistance to any type of discussion about their future plans had grated on him. No, she wasn't sure how to move forward with Liam, but she was very clear on one thing—she didn't want to lose him.

He emerged from the bedroom, his hair wet and slicked back from his face, still unshaven with a thick layer of stubble on his face. He was barefoot, shirtless, his chest hair still wet. The man *was* just sexy.

"Coffee?"

"That's exactly what I need, thank you." He walked past her—no kiss—and opened one of the kitchen cabinets and rifled through the bottles until he found the one he was looking for.

"Here you go." She put the coffee cup on the counter next to him.

Liam took out a bottle of ibuprofen, shook a couple of tablets into his palm, then popped them into his mouth.

"Aren't you supposed to get a headache before sex?"

He took a swig of coffee, wincing as the hot liquid hit the back of his throat. She could read him well enough now to know that he was irritated.

She put her cup on the kitchen butcher block island. "Look… I can tell that you're annoyed with me."

He put his cup down as well. "Not annoyed. Frustrated."

Same difference as far as she was concerned.

"Okay. Frustrated. And now I'm starting to feel frustrated with you and that's not how I want to feel."

Liam grabbed a T-shirt off the back of one of the bar stools and slipped it on over his head. Then he crossed his arms protectively in front of him as if he were gearing up for a fight. "What are you feeling frustrated about?"

"This obsession you seem to have about us moving forward." She used air quotations when she said *moving forward*. "We haven't even been together all that long. What's the matter with how things are now? I *like* how things are now. What's the big rush?"

"I already know what I want," Liam said. "I want you. I want to be with you. I want to wake up with you in the morning, I want to go to bed with you every night. And the fact that you don't want the same thing makes me question what the hell I'm doing in this relationship."

"You question why you're with me?" Kate asked, stung. "Just because I'm not jumping up and down at the thought of getting married?"

"You don't have to say it like it's a dirty word."

"I didn't."

"Yes. You did. That's the problem. You and I don't have the same vision for the outcome of what we've started here. I've never made it a secret that I want to be a part of a family. My *own* family. We could have that, you and me and Callie."

She gestured around her, to his cabin, to his homestead on Sugar Creek Ranch. "And what? Callie and I move here? You move to the Triple K? Change everything about our lives?"

Kate started to scratch at her neck, feeling hot and itchy all over her body.

"Just because things change doesn't mean it's for the worse. And to answer your question—I would leave Sugar Creek. For you."

Liam stared at her; watched her clawing at her neck. "Jesus," he said. "Just look at you. One conversation about marriage and you break out in hives."

"Don't be ridiculous," Kate snapped. "I don't have hives. And just so we're clear, you don't understand. I've got a lot on my plate right now. I've been looking into apartments for Callie in town. She wants to be independent and I want that for her. But Callie thinks that she wants to leave the ranch, but she has a really hard time with change."

"I do understand that. Either way, we can make things right for Callie." Liam pinned her with a pointed look. "Let's be honest. You have just as much difficulty with change as Callie. Maybe even more."

A tingle of fear raced up her spine—this wasn't at all how she expected their long-awaited afternoon of lovemaking to go. The silence stretched between them until it felt awkward that neither of them was saying anything.

Finally, she spoke what they both were thinking. "What if I don't want things to change? What if I like how things are?"

Liam pushed away from the island to put some distance between them, leaned back against the kitchen sink and crossed his arms in front of his body again.

"If we don't want the same thing, Kate, then we've got to end it now. That's not what I want. But we're not teenagers. We're old enough to know what we want."

Her fingers gripped the edge of the counter as she swallowed hard several times.

"Do you—" she started and then stopped "—want to call it quits right now?"

Liam stared at her hard, his eyes filled with disappointment. "Like I just said, that's not what I want. I want us to make a plan to be together for the rest of our lives. *That*'s what I want. But if what you're saying is that all you want is this—" he gestured between them "—casual arrangement where we get together on my days off to make love and I come over for dinner once or twice a week."

He paused and she waited.

"If that's what you're telling me, then, yes. We need to cut our losses and move on."

Two weeks went by without a phone call from Liam. Kate was so busy with the ranch and the horse training and looking at assisted-living apartments for Callie in town that she was able to put Liam out of her mind most of the day. But at night, especially during that block of time when she would crawl under the covers and call his number to talk about their days, that's when life without Liam really hurt. She missed him like he was a missing limb—he was gone, but she could still feel him.

So many times, she picked up her phone, stared at it, debating whether she should call him and break the silence. Yet she knew in her heart that she wasn't ready to commit *forever* to him. Not because he wasn't wonderful and worthy—he was. And it wasn't that she didn't love him, because she did. What it came down to, for her, was that she had built a life for nearly two decades. It wasn't a perfect life, but it was *hers*. She wasn't beholden to anyone, she didn't have to account for another person other than her daughter, and she was in complete control of her money and her future. Liam wanted a marriage, he wanted a wife. If she gave in to that future, how much of her own autonomy would she lose? How much of her life would remain her own?

For her, it was a big question. It was, in fact, *the* question.

"Fred." Kate found her most trusted employee overseeing the installation of new automatic waterers for the stalls.

"Yes, ma'am?"

"I need to leave the ranch for a while. Can you stay a little late today so Callie isn't here alone?"

Fred tipped his head. "Yes, ma'am."

Kate found Callie and let her know she was leaving before she headed out. She thought she should change her clothes—it'd been raining for days, so her jeans and boots were caked with mud. But it felt as if she didn't have the moment to spare; she didn't want to wait to get to Liam. Two weeks without him had been long enough. If he had been trying to show her what life would be like without him, his plan had worked. She discovered that, no matter what change was coming down the pike, she did not like her life without Liam Brand.

At Sugar Creek Ranch, Kate parked her truck next to his truck, rushed up the porch stairs of Liam's cabin and knocked on the door. This was his usual day off, but it'd been a risk driving all the way to his ranch without calling ahead, as she knew his schedule changed with the wind, it seemed. But she was in luck—Liam was home because all of his vehicles were accounted for.

After several minutes on his doorstep without any answer, Kate knocked again, a little harder this time. When there was still no answer, she tried the front door. Not surprising, it was unlocked.

"Liam?"

Kate left her boots on the front porch, not wanting to drag mud onto his clean floors. Then she stepped inside the quiet cabin and shut the door behind her.

"Liam?"

She didn't think to check the barn or the pasture to see if one of the horses was missing—he could very well be out riding or fishing. Her plan was to check the master bedroom, because Liam was known to nap during the day, and then investigate the barn, the pasture and the workshop.

"What the hell?" Liam walked out of his bedroom, naked.

Kate jumped, startled, and put her hand on her chest. "God! You scared me!"

"*I* scared you! I'm supposed to be here."

The horse trainer couldn't stop herself from looking at Liam's naked body, from his muscular arms, to his flat stomach, to his groin. She felt a tingling sensation between her thighs; she couldn't be around this man without thinking about making love with him. She'd never felt such a strong attraction to a man. Maybe that should've been a clue.

Liam stared at her for a moment, silently, before he

turned on his heel and went into his bedroom. He emerged a few minutes later dressed in jeans and a T-shirt, but he was still barefoot.

"I knocked," she explained, feeling out of place in his cabin now.

"I just woke up." Liam pulled the refrigerator door open and grabbed a beer. "You want something?"

Yes. You.

"No. I'm good. Thank you, though."

He twisted the top off his beer, tossed it in the sink and then took a long swig from the bottle.

"So—you're good, then?" he said after he swallowed.

That seemed to be a loaded question. He was asking her about much more beyond her level of thirst.

"Can we sit down?" she asked. Why was she feeling so nervous around him? What was there to be afraid of? This was Liam, after all. He loved her. But the man was such a highly sought after bachelor in their part of the world, it wasn't inconceivable that he could have moved on to greener, more commitment-friendly pastures.

He joined her on the couch, his expression sullen and guarded. Kate knew this man well enough to know that he had not fared well during their short separation.

"What's on your mind, Kate?" Liam hadn't smiled at her once since he discovered her standing in his living room.

"I…" She had to stop to gather her thoughts before she started over. "I've missed you."

He said nothing in return.

"I'm sorry," she added.

"No need to be sorry." There was a coldness, a distance in his deep voice that she hadn't heard before. "You can't change who you are or what you want."

"I think I can," she told him quietly. "I think I have."

Even those words didn't soften his expression; his mouth was drawn down, the expression in his eyes wary.

"I find that difficult to believe." Liam gave one shake of his head. "It occurred to me the other night—maybe I'm no different than one of your horses. You come over, you take me for a ride, and then you put me back in my stall until the next ride. Just because I'm a man doesn't mean I like feeling used."

Kate realized, right then and there, that she had pushed Liam to the limit. If she were going to turn this boat around, she was going to have to take charge and get it done. She stood, moved to the cushion next to Liam, took his beer bottle out of his hand, put it on the table and then took his hands in hers. She took it as a positive sign, a bright spot in an otherwise dark moment, that he hadn't pulled his hand away.

"I love you, Liam."

He didn't return the endearment.

"I know that I haven't always said it as much as you've wanted me to. But I do. Love you. And I've missed you more than I can express. If you wanted to show me what life was like without you—" she shrugged a shoulder "—it worked. I don't like my life without you now. *You* have become essential to me."

Liam's eyes roamed her face, lingering for the briefest of moments on her lips before his gaze returned to her eyes. It seemed like a really long time before he answered, and when he did, he, of course, had to throw her off balance.

"Are you saying this just because you want to get laid?"

Kate was stunned for a split second and then recovered, hit him on the shoulder and frowned at him. "Are you being serious right now? Because I'm being serious. I'm trying to say yes to you."

"You're saying yes to me?" Liam sat up straighter, bringing his body closer to her for the first time.

"Yes."

Liam took her face in his hands and kissed her lightly on the lips.

"You're saying yes to tomorrow?"

"Yes."

Another kiss.

"You're saying yes to forever?"

"Yes." Her voice was breathier now, her heart beginning to beat faster.

He kissed her neck.

"Are you saying yes to marriage?"

She hesitated for only a second before she nodded. "Yes."

Liam gathered her into his arms, her breasts pressed tightly against his chest, his tongue intertwined with hers.

"Are you saying yes to taking me for a ride?"

Kate laughed against his firm lips. "God, yes!"

Liam lifted her into his arms and carried her to his bedroom. They stripped out of their clothes and met each other, naked, in the middle of his bed. There wasn't much foreplay—he was hard and she was wet. They wrapped their arms and legs around each other's bodies, and he slipped deep inside her, and they found that rhythm that only they knew.

After the lovemaking, Kate curled her body next to the man she loved and felt like she had finally come home. Wherever Liam Brand was, as it turned out, *that* was home.

"Kate?"

"Hmm?"

"Did you just agree to be my wife?"

She tightened her hold on his body and nodded. "Yes."

"I'll have to get you a ring."

"Okay."

There was a span of silence and then he added, "And I'll have to actually propose."

"Whatever you want."

"I have what I want." He kissed her on the top of her head.

"So do I."

They lingered in bed for an hour and then Kate checked the time on her phone and realized that the day was slipping away, and she needed to get back to Callie. Liam watched her through sleepy eyes as she dressed.

"You're beautiful," he told her, his eyes drinking her in.

"You always say that."

"Because it's always true."

Dressed and ready to go, Kate walked around to his side of the bed and leaned down to kiss him. He accepted the kiss, but reached for her hand to stop her from leaving.

"Sit down for a minute. There's something I want to talk to you about."

There was a seriousness in his tone; this wasn't going to be a light conversation.

"I've been thinking a lot about us—and by *us* I mean, you, me and Callie. I know how much you worry about what would happen to Callie if something happened to you."

That was true. Her biggest worry had always been about her daughter. Who would take care of her? Who would watch out for her? If she had gotten a different father other than Lloyd in the father lottery, her worries wouldn't be so great. But that wasn't the case.

"I want to adopt Calico."

Kate was rendered temporarily speechless. Yes, Lloyd was an absent father, but he was listed on the birth certificate. She'd been a single parent for so long that it seemed more normal than not.

"Did you hear me?" Liam prompted her out of silence.

"I did." She gave a quick nod. "I just don't know what to say."

"You don't have to say anything right now. Just think on it. I know she's an adult now, but she's always going to need someone to watch out for her. That way, she'll have a full-time father and you'll have peace of mind that if something happens to you, Callie will have the entire Brand family looking after her."

Chapter Eleven

Kate did think about Liam's offer, and the more she thought about it, the more she came to believe that the idea made sense. Callie could have a large, powerful, wealthy family on her side for the rest of her life. And the truth was, if the laws of nature unfolded in a typical fashion, that Callie would outlive both of them. Liam had a pack of siblings—someone would be there to watch out for Callie. The Bozeman Brands stuck together like glue, and once Callie was a Brand, they would take her into the fold as one of their own.

The only roadblock to the entire plan was, of course, Lloyd. It had taken him weeks to return her phone call about Callie coming to see him, and she wasn't the least bit surprised when he came up with an excuse for why his daughter couldn't come for a visit. She really dreaded discussing adoption with him, because Lloyd, from what she could gather over the phone, hadn't matured a whole heck of a lot over the last several decades. He could still be jealous, petty and downright unreasonable.

"Katie Did!"

Kate cringed at the nickname and the sound of Lloyd's voice. This time, though, she didn't correct him as she usually would.

"Two weeks in a row. This's got to be some sort of record," he added.

"How are you, Lloyd?"

"Can't complain," her ex said. "Who'd listen anyway, right?"

"Right."

"Hey, Katie Did, I'm real sorry Callie can't come see me this year. What, with the economy just really starting to come back and construction picking up, I just can't…but next year, for sure."

"Sure," she agreed, but didn't put any stock in the idea. "Look, there's something I need to discuss with you."

A tense silence on the other end of the line.

After a moment, Lloyd cleared his throat. "Now, Katy Did, I know I owe you a couple of clams…"

Kate cut him off. "I'm getting married."

Another strained silence.

"Did you hear me?"

"Do I need to get my ears checked? Did you say you were getting married?" He sounded so surprised that it irritated her. Why was the idea of her getting married so shocking to him? Should she pine for him until death?

"Your ears work just fine." Kate struggled to maintain a civil tone with the man.

"Well, isn't that something? A big surprise," he continued. "I suppose congratulations are in order. Who'd you manage to slap that ole ball and chain on?"

"Liam Brand. You actually played ball with him in high school, I think."

"Yeah." Lloyd didn't sound impressed. "I know the guy."

More silence.

"Is that all?" he pressed her, seeming a little more impatient to end the call.

"No," she replied as evenly and calm as she could. "There's no real easy way to say this, so I'm just going to say it. Liam wants to adopt Calico, and I want him to adopt Calico, which means that you need to forfeit your parental rights."

"So, how'd he take it?" Liam had arrived at the Triple K for dinner and now, as was their habit, they had taken their coffee to the swing beneath the old oak tree in the front yard.

"The phone call went downhill fast after that."

Liam wasn't surprised; he hadn't liked Lloyd back when they played ball together. Kate's ex had always been a fast-talker who'd had an even faster fastball. Everyone thought he'd make the pros one day, but it seemed like Lloyd had fallen short of fulfilling all of his potential. Particularly when it came to his daughter, Callie.

"I hate the fact that Callie's father is such a jerk. But he *is*, in fact, a *jerk*! This isn't about him wanting Callie to be his daughter, because I think we're all pretty clear on his position on fathering her. And it's not like he has any feelings for me, other than some lingering, misguided, misplaced, sense of *ownership*. As if because he was the *first* one to gain access to my vagina that he has a lifetime guarantee or something!"

"He was your first?" Why did that even bother him in the slightest? And yet, irrationally, it did. Kate sent him a withering look, and he immediately regretted asking.

"God." She rolled her eyes in frustration. "Are all men a slave to your stupid egos? Who was your first, if we're asking questions?"

Liam opened his mouth, but before he could respond, she cut him off.

"Never mind. I don't care. And neither should you."

"I don't." He finally got a word in. "Just forget what I asked. I'm a man, and as such, I tend to say really stupid things. Friends?"

Kate rewarded him with a smile. "Friends."

They talked about a strategy to get Lloyd to sign over his parental rights. Their best bet was the thousands of dollars of back child support Lloyd owed; there was interest attached and the debt was only growing over time. If Lloyd agreed to sign over his rights so Liam could adopt Callie, they would find a way to settle that debt so Lloyd was free and clear.

"We won't talk to Callie until after we have the document in our hands," Kate insisted.

"Agreed."

"How do you think your kids will react? To you adopting Callie, I mean."

Liam had thought about his kids and Callie quite a bit. Even though things had eased between him and his kids by the end of their week together, their relationship had been damaged by the distance.

"I don't think Cole will care one way or the other, really. But Sarah… She's going to be upset about the marriage and the adoption."

"But she was so good with Callie," Kate said. "Why would she mind?"

"She was good with Callie and I was proud of her for that," he said. "She wants to come back to Montana."

"To live with you?"

Liam nodded. Sarah had nearly begged him to let her stay before they headed out to the airport. They had moved to a different part of Seattle to be closer to her stepfather's work, and she hated the school, she hated the new house, and she hated her mother for moving her away from friends and her home for a second time.

"I spoke with her mom last week. She's totally against the idea."

"Could we fight her?"

Liam had been looking out at the landscape, but now he wanted to look at Kate's face. The fact that she used the word *we* was very meaningful to him. For the first time, in a long time, he felt what it was like to have a woman standing by his side.

"It's not out of the question. But we've got to get ourselves straightened around first. We need to get things settled with Callie's father before we start dealing with my ex."

"One ex at a time."

"That's right," he agreed. "One ex at a time."

"Daddy!"

Kate was in the middle of treating an infection in one of her horse's hooves, bent over with her back aching, when she heard Callie scream in excitement. This, in itself, was not unusual. Callie could get over-the-moon excited about the smallest of things. *What* she screamed, however, was an entirely different thing.

Kate put the cap on the syringe she was using to treat the hooves, patted the horse on the neck and walked, quickly, toward the front of the barn. There, she found something she had never expected to find: Lloyd standing in front of her barn hugging Callie.

"Hello, Katie Did."

"Kate," she corrected for the umpteenth time in the last decade and a half.

"Mommy!" Callie had tears in her eyes. "Daddy's here!"

Lloyd, tall, slender, with more gray in his hair than black, was still a handsome man. When they met, he was in college and she was still in high school. Oh, how she had thought the sun rose and set because of Lloyd Harrison. Not to mention that he had the hottest muscle car in Bozeman. And, out of all the girls in town, Lloyd wanted her.

"You're lookin' good, Katie." Lloyd slipped off his glasses so she could see his green eyes. He knew how women loved his unusual cat eyes because he'd been told so often.

"Callie," Kate said in an even tone, "why don't you go on in the house and fix your father something to drink. You still like sweet tea, Lloyd?"

"The sweeter, the better." He winked at her.

God, she hated him.

"Go on, kitten," Lloyd said to Callie. "Mind your mother."

"I don't need your help in that department," Kate snapped at him. That was just like Lloyd. Show up, un-

announced, out of the blue, after years of avoiding the
Triple K like the plague, and try to take up the role as
a parent. He hadn't *earned* that right.

Kate waited until her daughter was out of earshot
before she narrowed her eyes at the wayward father of
her child. "*What* are you doing here?"

"Is there something wrong with a father coming to
see his daughter?"

"Yes," she barked at him. "If the father happens to
be you. Tell me why you're here."

"Now, Katie Did…there's no need to get all riled up."
Lloyd tried to use his charm on her. He added with a
condescending laugh, "Woo-we darlin'. You still have
one hell of temper on you, don't you?"

The man actually tried to put his arm around her
shoulders. She spun out from underneath his arm, wishing that she had a reason to shoot him. She might be
able to make a case for trespassing.

"You're *not* staying here, Lloyd. Get that straight
right now. Callie is going to ask, and you are going to
say 'no, thank you.'" Kate began to march toward the
house, her fists balled up next to her body. "God! I can't
stand the fact that you're here."

Lloyd just laughed at her frustration. She was convinced, after years of dealing with him, that the man
had zero ability to feel sympathy or empathy.

"Why are you so fired up, Katie Did?" Lloyd saun-
tered behind her, his long legs matching her stride one
for two.

Kate stopped in her tracks, spun on her heel and con-
fronted him. "I swear to God in heaven, Lloyd. If you
ever call me Katie Did again, I am going to shoot you
and bury your body in the compost pile!"

Lloyd, still smiling at her, held up his hands in surrender. "You've still got it, Katie. That spark that makes a man want to plug in. Lightning in a bottle."

Disgusted, Kate let her ex into her home, her private space. But only because he was Callie's father. Somehow, that gave him a pass.

Kate had to tolerate Lloyd sitting at her table, eating her food and breathing her air. She stared at him, arms crossed, while he ate like a man who didn't have one care in the world.

"Doggone, kitten." Her ex had polished off a huge plate of Callie's famous Polish sausage and sauerkraut. "You have turned out to be one heck of a cook, and that ain't no joke."

"Do you want more?" Callie asked.

Lloyd pat his stomach. "No, ma'am. I'm filled to the gills. But I thank you kindly."

"I—I'm glad you liked it."

When Callie took his plate to the kitchen, Lloyd leaned over and in a not-so-quiet whisper, he said, "I thought you were gonna do something about that stutter."

"Shut up." Kate stood, leaned toward him, put her hands flat on the table. "Shut. *Up!*"

Callie and Lloyd spent the rest of the day together while Kate buried herself in work. She knew exactly what this was about—her engagement to Liam. What else would bring Lloyd back to Montana after all of these years? He'd enjoyed her self-imposed spinsterhood. He took some pride in the fact that he had managed to spoil her for all other men.

She was hot and sweaty and smelled, as usual, like horse urine and manure. She found Callie and Lloyd sitting on the couch together, and her daughter was show-ing her father photo albums of when she was a baby and a toddler. It made Kate realize the days of photo albums were over. There were no photo albums of Callie when she was a teenager. All of the photos were cataloged on her computer, but she never looked at them. Not like Lloyd was looking at memories she created—memories he could have been a part of creating.

"How's it going in here?"

Callie was happy. No matter how much Lloyd made her skin crawl, her daughter was so happy to finally have her father visiting. She did not know, *could not* comprehend, why he had finally shown up now.

"We're having such a good time." Callie smiled at her broadly.

"That's right." Lloyd seconded the motion.

"I'm going to take a shower."

She locked her bedroom door before she stripped out of her dirty clothing. In the bathroom, she shut the door and locked that as well. Paranoid. But better safe than worrying that Lloyd might "accidentally" find himself in her bedroom.

Kate sat on the toilet, towel wrapped around her body, and dialed Liam's number for the third time. Frus-trated that he still didn't answer, she hung up without leaving a message. She sent him a text: Unexpected visitor. Please call as soon as you can.

In the shower, the horse trainer let the hot water beat down on her muscles, wishing that the water could wash Lloyd down the drain as easily as it was washing the dirt and grime from her skin.

But, alas, when she emerged from the bedroom, Lloyd was still sitting on her couch.

"Well—" he stood "—I suppose I should get going. I don't have a place picked out for the night."

"You can sleep here!" Callie, predictably, exclaimed. "On the couch."

"No, kitten. That just wouldn't be right."

His words said *no*, but his sad puppy dog expression said, *yes, I'd love to, thank you*.

"He can't stay here, Callie," Kate said firmly. "He's got things to do in town."

Disappointed, Callie said, "Well, at least stay for dinner."

Lloyd and Callie both looked at her expectantly. After a minute, she threw up her hands. "Fine. That's fine."

That's when Liam finally returned her call. She stepped outside, away from prying ears, and said, "Lloyd showed up this afternoon."

"He's there now?"

"Yes. How soon can you get here?"

Liam blew out a frustrated breath. "I've got a few more hours out in the field. Dammit."

"Will you come out after you're done? I don't care how late it is. I need to see you."

"I'll be there as soon as I can," Liam assured her. "And Kate."

"What?"

"Keep your cool."

Callie hugged her father good-night for the third time before Kate could get her to go on to bed. Her daughter was, understandably, afraid that she wouldn't see Lloyd for a long time.

"Good night, kitten." Lloyd leaned over a bit, that smooth smile in place, and blew his daughter an air kiss.

Kate heard Callie giggling happily as she shut the door to her bedroom. With a sigh, Kate went in to the kitchen to run the water over the dirty dishes to soak them before she rinsed them off.

She felt Lloyd come up behind her, so she shut off the water. Before she could turn around, Lloyd wrapped his arms around her from behind.

"I've missed us."

The feel of Lloyd's hands on her body, the feel of his breath on her neck, made her cringe. She didn't know why, couldn't explain it later, but instead of elbowing him in the gut, her body froze. She couldn't move. And that, of course, was the moment Liam opened her front door.

"Hello." The sound of Liam's voice spurred Kate into action. She wrenched herself away from Lloyd, who nonchalantly leaned back against the kitchen counter like he owned the place and had always belonged there.

"Lloyd was just about to leave." Kate made a beeline for her fiancé. "I'm so glad to see you."

She kissed Liam in greeting, wanting Lloyd to see her kiss her man, as if that would convince him that he didn't have a shot with her. Not that he really wanted a shot. What he wanted was to screw things up for her with Liam and then bail on her for a second time.

Thankfully, Liam hadn't misinterpreted the situation in the kitchen.

"Sorry I'm late." He actually apologized, and she knew that he was apologizing for the fact that he couldn't get there sooner.

"Liam, you remember Lloyd?"

After giving her another reassuring hug, Liam crossed the room to Callie's father. He offered Lloyd his hand. "Lloyd."

"Liam."

The handshake was brief, but the eye contact between the men lingered, as if they were sizing each other up.

"I'm surprised to see you here." Liam's eyes were narrowed.

"Likewise," Lloyd retorted.

"I'm here every week."

"Is that right?" Lloyd tucked his hands into his pockets.

"That's right." Liam wasn't smiling. "I know Kate told you about our engagement."

"She mentioned something like that."

"Are you hungry?" Kate wanted to change the conversation.

"Always." Liam smiled at her briefly before he turned his attention back to Lloyd.

"What brings you to town?" he asked her ex while she fixed Liam a plate.

"Just checking on my girls."

Kate glanced over to see Liam's features harden. "That's an interesting take on this situation."

"You don't say?"

"I do," Liam said in a sharp tone.

"Katie Did." Lloyd finally, thankfully, pushed away from the counter, set to leave. "Tell our daughter that I'll see her tomorrow."

Liam caught Lloyd's arm when he tried to pass by him. "You'd better plan on moving along, Lloyd."

The man laughed, but Kate heard a new nervousness

in that laugh. Liam had gotten to him and she was glad. Lloyd may have started this game, but she had no doubt that Liam Brand was willing to end it.

"Thanks for dinner." Lloyd gave her a little salute before he walked out the door.

Kate stopped what she was doing, walked over to Liam and hugged him tightly.

"Are you okay?" He kissed the top of her head.

"No." She shook her head. "Yes. I don't know."

Liam took her face in his hands. "We're going to handle him together."

She fed him, and they both agreed that he would spend the night on the couch. But after she made up the couch with a sheet, blanket and pillow, Kate realized that, tonight, this situation wouldn't do at all.

Liam moved past her to lay down on the couch, but she stopped him.

"I want you to stay with me. In my bed."

"Are you sure?" he whispered, not wanting to awaken Callie.

She nodded. "I'm sure."

Together, they walked down the hallway to her bedroom. Lloyd had tried to ruin her relationship with Liam, she was sure of that. But he had failed. Instead, he had pushed them closer together. And for the first time since high school, Kate felt as if she were finally free of Lloyd Harrison.

Chapter Twelve

The first night after Lloyd had arrived was the first night Liam stayed over at Kate's place, in her bed. They had made love in a slow, sweet, poignant way, different from any other time. And then he had held her until she got too hot and turned onto her side and away from him. For hours, he listened to Kate breathing in her sleep. He, on the other hand, hadn't been able to fall asleep at all that night. Lloyd's sudden appearance in their lives had thrown him into crisis mode—he didn't think Kate's ex had any power over their future relationship, but he did hold the key to a future adoption of Calico.

While Kate slept, Liam thought. He tried to think strategically, trying to anticipate Lloyd's next step. But it wasn't just the ex that had kept him awake—it was Kate's mattress, which had to have been manufactured around the time of the floods. It was lumpy, hard and there was a wayward spring poking him in the back. He hoped that she wasn't seriously attached to the monstrosity because after they were married, it was going to be the very first thing to go.

At the crack of dawn, and before Callie awakened, Liam snuck out of Kate's bedroom and made a pot of coffee. Kate and Callie, both ranch women, got up just as the sun was rising.

"Hi, Dr. B-Brand!" Callie greeted him with a smile and a hug.

"Good morning, Callie." Liam was standing at the stove, overseeing some scrambled eggs. "How am I doing so far?"

Callie looked concerned. "Not good at all."

Liam laughed, handed her the fork in his hand and stepped aside. Callie naturally took over in the kitchen while Liam and Kate went out to the barn. It was summertime and the Triple K Ranch was a huge spread, so most of the horses stayed out all day and all night. The horses still in the barn were boarded horses whose owners wanted them in at night.

Kate fed her barn cats, saying, as she always did, that she needed to get a kitten who would grow up to actually mouse the barn. After his fiancée checked to make sure that the stable hands had all arrived and were on track with her protocol for taking care of the animals, she had a minute to speak to him before he left to get started with his full day.

Kate wiped her hands off on her cutoff shorts. "Do you have a busy day?"

They were standing at his truck now.

He smiled down at her—she was so pretty, with that sun-kissed skin and sun-streaked hair that was escaping from her ponytail holder more than usual because of her recent haircut. Liam brushed some strands hair away from her forehead.

"Packed."

She reached for his hand; slowly, Kate was showing him more affection. And that incremental improvement in her ability to show her feelings for him bolstered his confidence in the future success of their marriage. He was a man who wanted the touch of his spouse. In fact, one of the biggest hallmarks of the failure of his last marriage was the fact that he chose a woman who wasn't physically affectionate.

"Did you sleep okay?"

"Baby—that mattress." He shook his head with a grimace. "I hope you're not attached."

She laughed. "No. There's just always something else around here that needs fixing. We can get a new one."

"All right. First potential marital crisis averted."

Another laugh. "I didn't snore, did I?"

Liam gave her a kiss on the lips. "Not much."

It was a rough day, the day after he spent the night at the Triple K Ranch. He lost steam around noon and had to gulp down several super-caffeinated drinks just to get through the day. Kate texted him to let him know that, despite their best hopes, Lloyd had returned to the Triple K to visit with his daughter. It took every ounce of his professionalism not to cancel his afternoon appointments and head straight back to the Triple K. What kept him on the job was the fact that Kate was a strong, savvy, capable woman who was smarter than Lloyd by a long shot; Liam had a lot of faith in his woman's ability to handle her ex. Between clients, he had asked his brother Bruce to get one of the Sugar Creek Ranch hands to take care of his horses for the next couple of weeks. He also called the family attorney to discuss the process of Lloyd relinquishing his parental rights and adoption of a special-needs adult. At the end of his day, he stopped by his cabin, threw some changes of clothing into a duffel bag and then hightailed it to the Triple K. If Lloyd was going to show up every day, then he was going to make sure he was on-site every day too. Was that naked, blatant male posturing? Sure. With a guy like Lloyd, if he didn't do it, it would signal to Kate's ex that things weren't so set in stone between them. Liam had every intention of "marking his territory."

That evening, when he arrived at the Triple K, Lloyd had already taken off. Liam was relieved because he was exhausted. He wasn't even really all that hungry, but he ate anyway just to spare Callie's feelings. While he ate, Callie talked ceaselessly about her day with Lloyd. It seemed that her father, for the first time, was trying to take an active role in his daughter's life. He took her out to lunch in town and then took her shopping for cooking utensils, the quickest way to Callie's heart. Liam had to admit he was impressed with Lloyd's game, but he wasn't impressed with the motives. Lloyd coming in at the eleventh hour to assert his rights had absolutely nothing to do with love for his daughter and everything to do with his overinflated ego.

After Callie went to sleep, Kate sat next to Liam on the couch and leaned her head on his shoulder with a heavy sigh.

"He exhausts me."

"I think that's the point."

"But Callie loves him. She loves him being here."

"I know." He took her hand into his. "But how is she going to feel if he pulls another decade-long disappearing act?"

"It will crush her," Kate admitted easily. "Again."

Liam lifted his head so he could look down into Kate's face. "We can't stop her from getting hurt. I wish we could. But we can make sure she had a really soft place to land."

Kate tilted up her chin so he could kiss her. They sat together, kissing, nuzzling each other, taking comfort in the other.

"I'm so tired," he told her. "I want to make love but…"

His woman shook her head. "Don't worry about it. I'm exhausted too. I just want to take a shower and crawl into bed."

Kate stood. "You can sleep with me again if you want. It worked out that you got up ahead of Callie."

Liam was willing to do time on that lumpy, spring-loaded mattress in order to be with Kate. If it made her feel better to have him next to her, then next to her was exactly where Liam was going to be. That was true love in his book.

Much to his and Kate's surprise, Lloyd stuck around for the entire week. What they had first initially dismissed as some sort of ego-driven gain, if it had begun that way, ended much differently for all of them.

"Are you okay?" Liam asked Kate, who was sitting across from him at the Nova Café where they could get all-day breakfast.

The papers for Lloyd to relinquish his parental rights to Callie were signed and a copy was in the glove box of his truck. Ever since they left his lawyer's office, ever since they had watched Lloyd drive his rental car away, Kate had been quiet and pensive. Not at all the reaction he had expected. Not at all the reaction he had *hoped* for.

She nodded, her face pale, her eyes worried and distant.

Liam leaned his forearms on the edge of the table, leaned forward so he could speak in a lowered, private voice.

"I can see that something's wrong, Kate," he told her. "Are you having buyer's remorse?"

Another shake of her head. It occurred to Liam that she hadn't hardly said more than two words beyond ordering her food.

"Tell me what's on your mind. I can't help if I don't know what's going on."

Suddenly, there were tears in Kate's eyes. He watched her stiffen her resolve and stop the tears from falling on to her cheeks.

"Do you want to go home?" he asked, confused. "I can take you home."

"No." She finally seemed to find her voice. "No. I don't want to go home."

Now that she was talking again, he wasn't going to interrupt. He waited for her to continue.

"I think I'm…shocked that it's finally over. I finally have what I want, and yet." She paused, seeming to search for the right words. "I don't feel happy about it. Why did I think it would be so easy? The father of my child just signed over his parental rights. It feels like the ground just shifted beneath my feet."

She had been looking at the window; now she was meeting his eyes again.

"But, there's a part of me that still can't believe that he agreed to give Callie away." Tears were swimming in Kate's wide eyes. "It hurts, Liam. I hurt so much for Callie."

Liam reached for her hand across the table.

"It's just a really big deal. That's all."

He nodded. It was a big deal. But he didn't necessarily understand her shock. Lloyd had been absent before Callie had even been born. He hadn't paid one cent of court mandated child support. No, that bill had been paid by Liam, and he was glad to have done it in order to secure Callie's future.

"Even after all you've been through with him, you're still shocked that he agreed? Is that it?"

Kate rearranged her silverware. "I don't know. I guess. A little. I mean, I know that he hasn't been in Callie's life, but to sign away his rights. That's *forever.* He can't take that back."

"Would you want him to?" he asked quietly, his stomach feeling unsettled by her reaction.

It took her longer than he would have liked to answer that question. "No. That's not it. I'm glad that we can move forward with our plan. I just can't understand anyone wanting to give Callie away. She's an angel on Earth."

Liam squeezed her fingers reasurringly. "I'm sorry he hurt you. I'm sorry he hurt Callie. But in the end, we've got to give him credit for finally doing the right thing for the both of you."

Liam had spent a week with Lloyd Harrison, and even though he had every reason to dislike the guy, he'd ended the week actually liking him. Lloyd was funny, laid-back in a devil-may-care way that was appealing for the rest of the world beholden to adult responsibility. Lloyd was the guy at the bar that everyone liked, but never expected him to show up on time or keep his word or pay back the money he owed. They guy was likable, that was just the truth. And by the end of the week, Liam had begun to appreciate the fact that Lloyd wanted to see for himself that Callie would be truly taken care of by him. Humans were complicated, and it didn't make sense that Lloyd would spend years avoiding his parental responsibilities, only to show up in the eleventh hour and actually act like a dad. Liam didn't understand it, but he had found a way to respect it.

"I can't begin to explain this to Callie," Kate said after a long pause. "This is something that has happened to her, and I can't explain it in a way she would understand."

"I know, baby." Liam kept on holding her hand. "But Lloyd will always be welcome in her life, that hasn't changed. Callie hasn't lost a father—she's gained one."

Several weeks following Lloyd's departure, Liam's relationship with Kate felt strained. He had decided to return to his cabin, under the guise of wanting to get the horses back into a routine, in order to give her some space. No matter how many times he asked if she was okay and she answered yes, the feeling between them was distant. He just couldn't seem to break through with her, and the only thing he could think to do was give her some space and let her come back to him. It made him feel powerless and unsettled, but what other choice did he have? Kate wasn't the type of woman to be pushed.

He went through his routine, did his work and was always available on the other end of the line when Kate needed him. Liam kept on being a steady, calm force in his woman's life, and finally, *finally*, his strategy paid off.

"Hi, there!" Kate was working with a new horse in the round pen. "I'll be done in a minute."

"Take your time." Liam hung his arms over the top rail of the round pen.

Kate was amazing to watch with a horse. She was an incredible, confident rider, but where she really shined was on the ground with these magnificent, powerful creatures. She was an expert in natural horsemanship, and he managed to learn something new from her every time he watched her work.

"She's a beauty," he said as Kate clipped the lead rope onto the mare's halter to lead her to a nearby pasture.

"She is," Kate agreed. "This is North Star. Just arrived yesterday."

"Is she one of yours?"

Kate let the mare go into a small pasture where she could acclimate to her new environment alone.

"I wish," the horse trainer said. "She's only here for training. But I'll love her while she's here."

Kate turned to him and kissed him on the lips. "Hi."

"Hi." He smiled at her, wondering why she had invited him to the ranch in the middle of the afternoon.

"There's something I want to show you."

"All right."

Kate climbed behind the wheel of one of her ranch trucks, and he climbed into the passenger side. Today, she was steering their relationship, and from the happiness he saw in her eyes when she saw him, he was looking forward to where she was taking them, literally and figuratively.

Using one of the many dirt road veins that crisscrossed the massive ranch, Kate drove them to a hill that overlooked the barn and the homestead. She parked and they got out of the truck. Hand in hand, she led him over to a peak of the hill. Liam was surprised to see how flat the top of the hill was—it appeared to have been graded sometime in the past.

"What do you think of this view of the ranch?" she asked him.

Honestly, Liam didn't think any piece of land could rival Sugar Creek land, but this view was mighty close. Even though it wasn't the highest hill on the property, it gave a person a bird's-eye view of the pastures and barn, and in the distance, those beautiful, craggy Montana mountains.

"It's hard to beat," he admitted.

Kate gave a slight nod. "It's going to be tough, you leaving Sugar Creek. Have you given much thought to that?"

He turned his body toward her. "That's all I've been thinking about since the day I fell in love with you, Kate."

He'd thought to live out his days on Sugar Creek. It had never occurred to him that he might fall in love with a woman with her own spread, a spread that was her bread, her butter, and her heart and soul. The Triple K *was* Kate King, and he knew that if he wanted to be with her, he would have to be the one to leave his home.

"It'll be an adjustment," he added. "But I wouldn't want it any other way. I love you, Kate. I love Callie.

Whatever is best for the two of you is going to be best for me."

She squeezed his hand at his words.

"Ten years ago, I was going to build a new home on this site."

"I thought it looked like it had been graded and leveled."

She nodded.

"I had an architect draw up plans for my dream home. I had the financing and permits in place. Then one thing after another happened with the barn—I ended up replacing the entire roof—and all of my dreams for building a new home got derailed."

She turned to face him. "What do you think about *us* building a new home up here together. We could either add on to my plans or scrap 'em and design our perfect home together. Either way, we'll have enough space for your children."

Liam looked around, imagining a home on this hill. Imagining a home with Kate as his wife, Callie as his daughter and enough room for his children to visit or to live permanently.

"What do you think?" she prodded him impatiently.

Liam looked down into her expectant face. "I think this feels like home."

They embraced on that hilltop, their future as a family sealed with a kiss. Then, they stood side by side, arm in arm, both quietly imaging the house that would be built on the land where they stood.

"I'm sorry I've been so…" Kate paused, seemingly to find the right word. "Distant."

He didn't dispute her claim. She had been distant.

"I had some stuff to work through I guess."

"I'm just glad you're back."

Once again she turned to face him. "I am back, Liam. I'm back for good. I'm back forever, if you'll have me."

Was he mistaken, or did this sound like a proposal coming from his independent, commitment-phobic lady?

"What are you driving at, Kate?"

"I'm sorry that I didn't get here as fast as you did. You've always been so certain about me—about us. I just had to take a slightly longer route, that's all. But I know what I want, Liam. I'm not fuzzy about it. I'm not confused about it. I just know what I want for me and for Callie."

He waited for her to continue.

"Will you marry me, Liam? I don't want a big cere-mony. I don't want a dress or even an engagement ring. I just want to start our lives together."

He kissed her, long and deep. "I want that too."

"Then let's go to the courthouse and just do it."

This was something he hadn't thought about. He had a big family, and even though he hadn't shared the news of the engagement with them yet, they would be mighty hurt if they couldn't be there for the ceremony.

"That's not going to sit well with my family."

Kate frowned. "I know. I thought about that. But shouldn't *our* family come first? The sooner we get married, the sooner we can start with the adoption."

She had him there. When push came to shove, the family he was building with Kate had to come first. And he couldn't disagree with her logic—once they were married, they could go full steam ahead with the adoption.

"When?" he asked her.

"We could get the license this week. We'll have to tell Callie, of course, but I think she'll be happy. She's always been such a romantic."

"I can meet you in Bozeman tomorrow around noon."

A light touched his love's eyes, and it warmed his heart to see it.

"We're getting married." Kate flung her arms around him with an enthusiasm that he had never experienced with her before.

"I love you, Kate King." Liam hugged her tightly, kissing her cheek. "It seems like I've waited a lifetime for you."

"I love you." She rested her head over his heart, holding on to him as tightly as he was holding on to her. "God only knows how much."

Chapter Thirteen

They were married on a rainy Wednesday morning by Judge Harlow at the Bozeman city hall. They did it quietly and alone, without any fanfare or fuss. They had debated bringing Callie with them, but ultimately decided that they would celebrate the union at Sugar Creek Ranch with both of their families, and a handful of close friends, sometime over the following several weeks. The ceremony, as it were, would be just quick, painless and just for them.

And since this was for them, they wanted to dress how they lived—casual and ready for the barn. They did put on clean, new jeans, with shined-up boots. But they weren't fancy people, so their outfits for the wedding weren't fancy either. Holding hands, the newly married couple burst out of city hall and into the rain.

A fat drop of rain splatted on Kate's nose before she had a chance to put her cowgirl hat back on.

Liam swung her around and into his arms. Right there, on the city hall sidewalk, in the rain, Liam Brand kissed her for the second time as her husband.

"It's raining!" Kate laughed, not really caring that she was getting wet.

Liam picked her up and spun around. "Frankly, Mrs. Brand, I don't give a damn!"

They kissed again before racing to Liam's truck. Inside the cab, they were dripping on the seats, their shirts and the thighs of their jeans soaked to the skin. But they were laughing. Kate couldn't have known—how could she have known?—just how happy she was going to be to say that she was Mrs. Liam Brand.

"Happy?" Liam asked her, rainwater dripping down his neck.

"Yes," she said with a happy, relieved sigh. "You?"

"This is, hands down, one of the happiest days of my life."

It was the nature of their lives that they had to part ways after the ceremony. She had a horsemanship clinic scheduled at the Triple K later on that afternoon, and Liam's schedule only allowed him to take a half day off.

"I'll see you tonight," he promised her with a kiss.

"It's our wedding night," she mused. She'd never made love to a husband before.

"Trust me." His eyes lingered on her lips. "I'm not going to miss it."

"You'd better not." She hopped out of the truck and said right before she shut the door, "I'll hunt you down if you do!"

* * *

All day, Kate's mind would drift back to the moment that she said "I do" to Liam Brand. She was *married*. It was unconventional, perhaps, and a little bit secretive. But she liked it that way. The only regret she had was for their children—Callie, Sarah and Cole still needed to be informed of the marriage, and she suspected that it was going to be a bumpy ride on Liam's end. And, yes, they still needed to tell their friends and Liam's large, extended family. Those were adults, and they could handle the disappointment. Or not.

Normally, she loved her horsemanship clinics. Today, she just wanted to get to the wedding night with Liam.

"Nice work everyone!" Kate was standing in the center of the covered round pen. "I'll see you next time!"

One by one, her clients bade her farewell. Some boarded on her property and didn't have far to go. Others had trailered their horses in, and she would make herself available in case of any loading issues. Kate was overseeing the last horse loading into the last trailer when Callie joined her.

"Hi, Mommy."

"Hi, kiddo." Kate gave her daughter a quick side-hug before she refocused her attention on the large, bay gelding loading on the trailer. "Give me just a minute, okay, Callie?"

"Okay, Mommy."

Callie knew to stand out of the way while she worked with the skittish horse. It took some doing, but they finally coaxed the gelding into the trailer with some sweet feed; the owner closed the doors of the trailer and shook her hand.

"We'll see you next month."

Once the last client was heading down the drive, Kate turned her attention back to daughter.

"What's up, kiddo?" Kate put her arm around her daughter's shoulders as they walked together.

"Tony asked me to come for a visit."

"In California?"

"Yes." Callie nodded. "He lives in San Diego with his mom and his dad."

Kate's stomach clenched. Whenever she thought of entrusting Callie to someone else, it made her feel tense and sick in the stomach. She recognized that this wasn't a sustainable position, not for someone like Callie who had a dream of her life that extended beyond the Triple K. Understanding this didn't make it any easier.

"When?"

"I—I don't know. Whenever I—I can make i-it, I—I think."

"I'll need to talk to Tony's parents," Kate warned.

"Okay."

"And we need to think about you visiting when I can fly out there with you. You can't fly alone."

"I—I know."

"I'm not saying yes." Kate tried to moderate Callie's expectations.

"B-but, you aren't saying no."

Damn, but she did have a point. "I'm not saying no."

That sent Callie running off toward the house shouting that she had to call Tony right away. Liam had changed her—he really had. Would she have so easily entertained the idea of Callie visiting Tony before her time with Liam? It was hard to imagine. Things had changed for her; she didn't feel like she had to have such a death grip on all things in her life in order to keep things from unraveling. It seemed that God had sent her the exact right man, at the right time in her life, to help her through a time of transition with her daughter. Thankfully, God had sent her Liam.

That night, they went through the motions—they sat down for dinner with Callie, cleared the table, washed the dishes and then watched TV together until Callie finally went off to bed. Like two teenagers, they rushed down the hall, careful to be quiet as they sneaked past Callie's door, until they reached the master bedroom. Kate closed the door behind them and locked it.

"It's about damn time." Liam pulled her into his arms to kiss her the moment they were safe behind a locked door.

Kate returned his kiss with the same force, the same passion, her arms around his lean waist, her fingers massaging the long muscles of his back.

"Hello, Mrs. Brand."

"Hmm." Kate leaned back against his arms and smiled up at him. "That sounds right."

"Yes, it does."

They opened the blinds so the light from the nearly full moon would shine into the room after they turned off the bedside lamp. Not wanting to wait a minute longer to consummate their marriage, they both stripped out of their clothing without any fanfare. Liam was hard and ready to go. He grabbed her hand and led her to the bed; she resisted.

"I've been working all day. I'm dirty."

Liam nuzzled her neck. "I like dirty."

She laughed louder than she intended to. "Shh."

"Let's get into bed." He started to walk forward, walking her backward toward the bed.

"No." Kate put the brakes on. "You're going to want to kiss me down there, and I've been working all day. I've got to get into the shower."

"Want company?"

"Uh-huh."

He kept right on kissing her on the neck, on the breasts, his hands roaming her body, the feel of his erection, so hard and ready for her.

"Come on." Kate spun out of his arms. "Shower first."

She got the shower running, turning the hot water on full blast, and they both climbed into the tub and pulled the shower curtain closed.

"You'll have to whisper. There's an echo in here," Kate said quietly.

He was back to kissing her neck, licking the water off her skin as the water ran over their bodies. Unable to resist, she wrapped her hand around his hard shaft, loving the sound of Liam groaning with pleasure. It made her feel powerful.

Liam spun her around, his back to the water, wrapped her up in his arms, one hand covering a breast, the other hand between her thighs. His finger found that most sensitive part of her body and worried the little nub until her knees began to buckle and she had to bite her lip to stop herself from making too much noise.

"I need to get cleaned up," Kate said in a breathy voice. "I can't wait any longer, Liam."

Liam took charge, as he often did, and she let him. He soaped up his hands and cleaned her body, his slippery hands touching her everywhere. Her husband saved washing between her thighs for last.

"Oh, God." Kate had to hold on to him it felt so good.

"That was loud." He chuckled under his breath.

"Well, what do you expect with what you're doing to me?" she whispered and then gasped when she felt his finger inside her.

"I'm clean enough," she said urgently.

"Are you sure?"

"Take me to bed, Liam!" Kate whispered the demand.

With a quiet laugh, Liam let the water rinse the rest of the soap from her body, shut off the water, stepped out of the tub and grabbed a towel. When he tried to dry her off, she pulled the towel out of his hands and ran into the bedroom.

Along the way, she dried herself off as best she could, but parts of her body were still damp when she yanked back the covers and climbed on top of the cool, cotton sheet.

"Hurry up!" she whispered harshly.

In the soft light of the moon, Liam walked into the bedroom, tall, lean, muscular. This was her man. This was her husband. And she was so in love with him.

Liam's body was still damp as he climbed into bed beside her.

"I'm glad to be here with you, baby." Her husband leaned over her and kissed her nipple.

"I'm so glad you're here."

"Are you cold?" he asked.

"No," she said urgently. "Horny."

"I can help you with that, Mrs. Brand." Liam ran his hand down over her breast, along her stomach and across her thigh. "You know where I want to start, right?"

"Yes." She nodded, letting her thighs fall farther apart.

His hands cupping her bottom, Liam knelt between her thighs and covered her with his mouth. He always treated her like the best dessert a man could have— licking her, kissing her, until she was squirming and writhing and digging her fingernails into his skin.

"Baby? Can you come like this?"

"I don't know," she gasped, wishing he hadn't stopped. "I don't think so. I just… I just get too tense. I worry about you… I worry…"

"Don't worry about me. I'm loving this. You're mine. You were made with me in mind. Just relax, baby, and enjoy it."

"Stop talking!"

Liam loved her with his mouth until all she could feel was the sensation of his tongue and his lips at the center of her being. That's when she let herself go. This was her husband loving her. She trusted him. Kate felt herself starting to orgasm; she held on to Liam, biting her lip to stop herself from crying out. She was panting and sweaty and so sensitive between her legs that she could hardly stand it.

"Yes, baby," Liam murmured.

"Please." Kate reached for him. "Please."

Her husband kissed his way up her body until they were chest to chest; then he reached between their bodies and guided himself inside. He caught her moan of pleasure in his mouth as he kissed her.

"I love you," she gasped. "God, I love you."

"I love you, baby." Liam used his body to tease her,

stroking long and slow, making her wiggle beneath him and beg him for more. Beg him to go deeper, go faster, love her harder. But her husband had other plans for her. He set the rhythm, took his time, driving her mad until he felt her tensing around him.

"There it is," Liam said in a silky, sexy voice. "I feel you coming for me."

All Kate could do was cling to her husband, bite down on his shoulder to keep silent as an intense second orgasm sent sparks firing from the center of her body outward.

He held her, was there for her, until she relaxed into his embrace. That's when he gave it to her deeper, faster, and loved her harder. It was wild and intense the way Liam loved her that night. It was a first for them, and certainly a first for her. It was if he wanted to consume her, heart, mind, body and soul.

Forgetting to be quiet in his release, Liam drove into her one last time, his arms locked and tense, and found his release.

Kate pulled him down on top of her and pulled the covers over their bodies. "Shh! That wasn't quiet at all."

Under the covers, their bodies still intertwined, they held each other tightly, kissing and laughing as quietly as they could.

"How was that for you, Mrs. Brand?"

Their bodies naturally fell away from each other and he lay on his back, while she used his arm as a pillow.

"I think I had three orgasms. *Three.* That's a record."

"That's great for my ego."

"Good." Kate hugged him. "There's something about making love as a married woman that just does it for me."

"Married sex is the best," Liam agreed.

They fell asleep in each other's arms; somewhere along the way, Liam had slipped out of the room and bedded down on the couch. Before they fell drifted off to sleep, they both agreed that they would have to sit down with Callie soon. And as far as the Brand family was concerned, Sunday brunch was as good a time as any to let them know that they had gotten married.

The first person they told about their marriage was Callie. Understandably, she was upset that she hadn't been able to be a part of the ceremony. Mainly, she had wanted to get a new dress, new shoes and maybe catch the bouquet as a sign that she would marry Tony. Liam planned on telling his father, stepmother and siblings first, and then right after brunch, call his kids. That wasn't a phone call he was looking forward to making. When they were in Montana, neither of them really warmed to the idea of Kate. Which didn't make a bit of sense, in light of the fact that their mother had left him and had remarried over a year ago.

Sunday brunch was a loud affair, as per usual. His family was boisterous, opinionated and often talked over each other. He waited until most of the food was gone—his father often handled things better on a full stomach.

"Ready?" Liam asked Kate.

She nodded.

"Ready?" he asked Callie, who had been very good at keeping their secret.

Callie's eyes lit up and she nodded definitively. "Yes!"

"All right, then." Liam stood.

"Can I have your attention everyone?" He had to shout over his siblings.

"Will you guys shut it?" Jessie, Liam's sister, shouted. "Liam's got something to tell us!"

"Jessie—" Lilly's steady voice cut through the noise, as it always did "—that's not the way I raised you to act."

Jessie backed off, because Lilly did rule the roost, but she pointed to her siblings. "It's their fault! They're rude, so I have to be rude."

"What's got you out of your chair, Liam?" Jock bellowed. His father spoke only in a shout.

"Let Liam speak," Lilly commanded in her calm way.

There was one person to whom all of Jock's children deferred and that was Lilly. The table went silent and suddenly everyone's attention was on him.

"Many of you know how I feel about Kate and Callie." Liam reached for his wife's hand. "I haven't been this happy in a long, long time. I asked Kate to marry me."

His family wasn't quiet after that announcement. A flurry of congratulations flew around the table.

"Actually, I asked you," Kate reminded him.

"Well, technically, I asked you first and then you asked me."

"Have you set a date?" Lilly's voice cut through the noise again.

"Yes." Liam nodded. "We have. Yesterday."

That stumped his family for a solid second or two before they all started to talk at the same time again.

Liam tugged on her hand to get her to stand up. "I'd like to introduce you to my wife, Kate!"

Then he took Callie's hand and encouraged her to stand up with them. "And my daughter, Calico."

Standing there, a proud husband and father, with two of his best girls on either side, Liam couldn't remember a time when he felt more content with his life. The only piece missing was moving forward with the adoption so Calico was officially his daughter. Then their picture would truly be complete.

"You're married?" Jessie, loud like their father, slammed her palms on the table. "How could you go and get all married without us!"

"It was the right thing for *us*." Liam eyed his siblings, sending them a silent signal to just deal with the news.

"Welcome to the family." Lilly came to the other side of the table to hug Kate and Callie.

"You know we're going to have to have a party, right?" Savannah made the rounds hugging each of them. "Call me later today, and we can start putting something together."

Jessie threw herself at Kate, almost knocking her down. "You must be certifiable to marry into this crazy family. Welcome to the fam."

"Don't strangle her, Jess," Liam joked with his sister.

"Sorry." Jessie gave his wife a sheepish look. "That's just how I hug."

All in all, the announcement had gone better than he'd anticipated. His family liked Kate and Callie, and liked them with him, so it wasn't such a big shock after all. Everyone agreed that they would have one heck of a reception and that way the entire family would have a chance to celebrate the union.

The dining room cleared, and as it happened, Liam was left alone with his stepmother, whom he had called mom since he was a youngster. His own mother had died when he was just a boy. Lilly, so kind and caring, was the only mother he had ever really known.

Liam kissed his mother on the cheek. "Do you like her?"

Lilly sent him a gentle smile. "Yes, I do."

"But," she continued. "Do you know what I like even more?"

He shook his head.

"I like how happy she makes you." Lilly touched his arm. "I have prayed for this, Liam. I am so grateful that my prayers have been answered and you have been blessed with such a lovely wife and daughter."

Chapter Fourteen

"What do you think?" Kate had been putting off the question of California until after they had shared the news of the marriage with all of their family members.

Perhaps she was just avoiding the topic, but now it was front and center once again. At dinner, Callie brought it up. Tony had called, and really, the topic of this trip was the only thing the two of them talked about. This wasn't going away.

"Have you talked to Tony's parents?"

"Not yet." Kate took a sip of her coffee. "I suppose I'll have to."

"It's not going away."

"That's exactly what I thought tonight. It's not going away."

Liam reached for his hand, which was his way.

"Our daughter will not be contained," he said. "She's

got bigger plans for herself than anyone, even you, imagined for her."

It warmed her heart to hear Liam refer to Callie as "our" daughter. He loved Callie as his own, and Kate had a feeling that she was going to have to lean on Liam pretty heavily during this next phase of Callie's life.

"I know." Kate sighed. "Why couldn't she have been content here on the ranch?"

"Then she wouldn't be Callie."

He was right. She knew he was. But it still hurt. Her daughter wanted to leave the ranch; her daughter wanted to leave her. She wasn't ready for it, but Callie was ready to flap her wings and fly out of the nest.

"Just do it and get it over with," Liam added. "The quicker you get it done, the better you'll feel."

He was on a roll with that being right thing.

"I'll set up a video chat with them," she said after a moment. "You'll do it with me, won't you?"

"Of course. All the parents have to get along, isn't that what you said?"

"That's the way it works."

"All right, then. We'd better start getting along with these folks. I've seen the way Tony and Callie look at each other, Kate. It looks like the real deal to me. They love each other."

"Hello, Mr. and Mrs. Salviano." Kate sat stiffly next to Liam.

"Please—call us Tottie and Tony Sr."

"I'm Kate and this is my husband, Liam."

"It's so nice to finally meet you." Tottie smiled at her with a toothy, super-white smile. She had a tanning-bed tan, salon-blond hair and she was draped in very expensive jewelry paired with casual designer clothing.

"Hi, Mrs. S! Hi, Mr. S!" Callie was wiggling next to her, hands clasped, so excited that her mom was finally talking to Tony's parents about the trip to California.

"There's Callie! Hi, sweetheart."

Kate watched Tony's parents closely. Both of them, as much as she hated to admit it, were very kind and accepting of Callie. They approved, at some level, to the match between Tony and Callie.

"Where's Tony?" Callie leaned forward as if getting closer to the screen would make Tony appear.

"He had to go to work, sweetheart. He wanted us to make sure that we tell you hello."

"Hello!" Callie bounced a little in her chair.

"Kiddo, why don't you groom Visa. He's caked with mud."

Her daughter waved goodbye to the Salvianos, tilting her head sideways. "Mommy wants privacy."

Kate waited until Callie had shut the front door behind her before she said to Tony's parents, "I had no idea when I signed her up for that online support group that she would…"

"Fall in love?" Tottie completed the sentence.

Kate nodded.

"I know it," Tottie agreed with a relieved expression on her face. "It was a shock for us too."

"We thought it might fade with time," Tony Sr. added.

Kate put her hand on her chest. "So did I."

The four of them spoke for almost an hour; even though they came from very different lifestyles and parts of the country, they all agreed that Callie and Tony needed to slow things way down between them. Tony's parents confirmed that he was, indeed, talking about proposing to Callie. And, on her end, she knew that Callie wanted to say yes. By the end of the conversation, Kate felt much more comfortable with the idea of Callie visiting the Salvianos in California for a week or two.

"When am I—I going to California?" Callie asked for the third time while they were cleaning up the dishes from dinner.

"Callie," Kate said evenly. "What did we talk about earlier?"

"That I—I have to wait."

"And...?"

"And you liked Mr. and Mrs. S."

Kate dried her hands on a dish towel and hugged her daughter. "I did like them. Very much. And I like Tony."

"I-I'm going to California."

Kate kissed the top of her daughter's head. "Yes, kiddo. You're going to California."

"B-by myself."

"Well, you won't be flying by yourself. I'll have to fly with you."

Her daughter frowned. "Why can't I—I go b-by myself?"

"Because you'll have difficulty getting around the airport once you land," Kate reminded her. Callie got very confused when it came to following directions, especially when there were crowds and lots of noise.

"B-but you aren't staying?" This was a question as much as a statement.

It hurt a little, this desire that her daughter had to separate from her. But, on the other hand, typically developing kids would have gone through this in their tweens and their teens. She at least got a couple extra years with Callie close by her side.

"Did you finally get to talk to Sarah and Cole?"

They had both been too worn out to make love; they lay in bed together, the lights off, the curtains open, talking. Liam had been having a difficult time getting his kids on the phone at the appropriate moment. They were with their mom or with their friends.

Liam wiped his hand over his face with a sigh. "I did."

"Oh." Kate sat up in a cross-legged position and faced her husband. "That doesn't sound good."

"No." He shook his head. "It didn't go well at all."

"Tell me what happened."

"Cole's not upset. He likes Seattle—he doesn't mind his new school. Of course, he has a lot more freedom than Sarah. He's older. But he's also a lot easier going about things than Sarah. She takes things to heart and Cole doesn't."

"What did Sarah say about the marriage and the adoption?"

"Once I saw the way she reacted about the marriage, I didn't say anything about the adoption."

"That bad, huh?"

"That bad."

They were both silent for a moment; everyone wanted family and friends to be happy about their marriage. That was human nature. It felt *uncomfortable* when folks weren't happy.

"I think…" Liam said, "that Sarah believes that my marriage to you means that she's stuck in Seattle and she'll never be able to come home to Montana."

"But that's not true." Kate put her hand on her chest. "At least not on our end."

"I told her that. But words are cheap with Sarah these days. She knows her mom is in control, and her mom wants her to stay in Seattle. Now that I'm married, Sarah figures there's no way her mom will agree with letting her come live with me."

Kate lay back down beside Liam, her hands resting on her stomach. They were both caught up in their own thoughts, not speaking.

"We have got to do something about this mattress," Liam grumbled, shifting uncomfortably.

Kate popped up again. "Let's switch. I'm used to the spring."

Liam reached for her and pulled her back down. "No. Come back here."

She lay back down, but the minute her head hit his shoulder, an idea came to her and she popped back up.

"What are you doing now?"

Kate went back to sitting cross-legged and facing him. "I just had a great idea."

"What's that?"

"We haven't even talked about our honeymoon."

"We've been so busy, with your back-to-back clinics and my exploding practice. I feel real bad that we haven't—"

"No," she said, cutting him off. "I wasn't trying to make you feel bad. I had an *idea*."

"Okay." Liam laughed. "You're so damn cute, Kate. Tell me your idea."

She touched his leg. "I love your laugh. Okay. Why don't we honeymoon here? We can both clear our calendars for two weeks. I'm actually kind of light next month. And, *then*, we can invite Sarah for a special trip to the Triple K. If she's here with us, we'll be able to *show* her that our marriage isn't a bad thing for her."

"You want my daughter on our honeymoon?" Liam sounded surprised and touched.

"Why not? Like you've said, we aren't teenagers. We both have children, and we need this marriage to work for everyone in our family, not just us."

Liam pulled her down playfully on top of him and kissed her. "Have I told you lately that I love you, Mrs. Brand?"

"No." Kate rested her head on his chest, listening to the steady, strong beat of his heart.

Liam ran his hands over her back.

"I love you."

"Oh!" Kate exclaimed. "Itch. Itch!"

Her husband started to scratch all over her back until she stopped squirming.

"Did I get it?"

"Yes! Thank you." She went back to resting on him. "I love you too, Liam."

They lay together, enjoying the quiet of the night, not feeling the need to fill every minute between them with talk.

Sleepily, Liam asked her, "Are we still too tired to fool around?"

Kate rolled off his body and curled into a ball facing away from him. "Yes."

"Okay," he agreed. "Kate?"

"Hmm?"

"We're buying a damn mattress tomorrow."

* * *

"How did you manage to get all of this done so quickly?" Kate couldn't believe that Savannah had managed to transform the main house of Sugar Creek Ranch into a wedding reception extravaganza. There was a band, and catered barbecue, and a photographer there to capture candid moments for a keepsake photo album.

"I was worried you wouldn't like it." Savannah looked around at the decorations with a critical eye. "Is it too fussy?"

"No. Not at all!" Kate was more than amazed, she was touched to her core. The Brand family was showing, by way of this party, that they were welcoming Callie and her with open arms.

"Then, I'm relieved." Savannah smiled, then her expression changed as her hand went to her noticeable baby bump. "My baby just gave me one heck of a kick! Must approve of the music."

Kate laughed feeling lighthearted and safe with her new family. "Do you know if you're having a boy or a girl yet?"

Savannah's face softened, her eyes filled with love for her unborn child. "A girl. We're having a girl."

She put her hand on her sister-in-law's arm. "Girls are so much fun. Any names picked out?"

"Amanda," Savannah told her. "After her great-great-aunt who came here for a visit with her father from South Africa and ended up falling in love and marrying into the Brand family. Family legend has it that Amanda Brand was a hard-as-nails trailblazer with a can-do, never-quit attitude."

"Amanda Brand." Kate tried out the name on her tongue. "I like it. I like it a lot."

* * *

It was moments like these that Liam appreciated his family the most. Yes, they were a large bunch, a rowdy opinionated bunch, with family dysfunction to spare. But the Bozeman Brands could pull together like no other family he'd ever seen. When someone was in need, they circled the wagons.

"Thanks for this, Pop," Liam said. "This is the kind of welcome I wanted for Kate and Calico."

"You've got Lilly and Savannah to thank," Jock said in his typically gruff tone. "I thought we could just throw a couple of steaks on the grill and call it a day."

Jock eyed him. "I was none too pleased to hear that you're abandoning the family."

That comment threw Liam for a loop. "What are you talking about, Pop? I'm not abandoning anybody. Certainly not my family."

"You're movin' right off of Sugar Creek. That's abandonment right there."

Jock wanted all of his children to live at Sugar Creek Ranch. Anything short of that was seen as a failure to him.

"Pop…come on."

"What do you think you're gonna do with that chunk of land I gave you? You're just gonna let it sit there and rot?"

"No." Liam put his empty glass down on a nearby table. "I'll keep it maintained. Sarah may want to live there when she's older."

"What about Cole? That ain't right takin' your son's birthright and handin' it over to Sarah."

"Pop. Cole isn't a rancher. Trust me. Out of the two of them, I think Sarah has Sugar Creek in her blood."

"The girl." Jock frowned.

Liam smiled, half in humor and half in resignation. His father was nothing if not a chauvinist. "Yes, Pop. The girl."

They ended the conversation with Jock handing him an envelope. "That's just a little fun money."

"Thank you, Pop. We appreciate you."

Jock waved off his comment like he was swatting away a pesky fly and then ended the conversation by just turning and walking away.

He was still watching his father when Kate appeared at his side.

"Can you believe all of this?" She looped her arm through his. "They even have a cake. A *wedding* cake. I didn't even realize that I wanted one until I saw it. Did you see it?"

"Not yet." Liam handed her the envelope. "This is from the folks."

Kate stared at the envelope for a moment before she peeked inside. She looked at the number on the check, her eyes widening slightly. She closed the envelope. "There's enough in here to revise the plans on the house *and* break ground!"

"Pop's always been generous with money." Liam nodded, not surprised. His father had always been generous with his money and his land—he just didn't have it in him to be generous with his praise.

Jock could always put him in a weird mood—it seemed that he could never really please Jock, and he wished his father's approval didn't still matter to him.

"May I have this dance?" Liam asked his bride, wanting to shake off his sullen mood. This was a night for celebration, not for an analysis of his complicated relationship with his father.

The moment he took Kate in his arms to slow dance to one of his favorite Trace Adkins songs, Liam forgot about everything as his focus narrowed to his wife's pretty face.

"Are you having a good time?" he asked her.

There was so much love for him, for his family, in her eyes when she said, "This is one of the best nights of my life, Liam. I'll never forget it."

He kissed her lightly on the lips, a promise of better things to come when they were alone.

"You look beautiful tonight, Kate." Liam was so happy to have her in his arms.

"I think you are so handsome." His wife gazed up at him in a way that made him feel completely accepted and loved. "I love looking at you."

Liam kissed her again with a chuckle. "That's good, baby. Because you're going to be looking at this mug for the rest of your life."

They danced and they drank and they ate incredible food together. They mingled with friends and family, and spent special time with Callie. Liam made sure that he had requested one of Callie's favorite songs so they could share their first father-daughter dance. At the end of the evening, when too much food and too much booze was consumed by all, it was time for the cake-cutting ceremony.

"Speech! Speech!" A chant started with the small gathering of friends and family.

Liam put his arm around Kate's shoulders, proud to call her his wife. Proud to call Callie his daughter.

He waved for Callie to join them from the front row

of the crowd. Shyly, she walked to his side, and he put his other arm around her shoulders so he was sandwiched in between mother and daughter.

"Thank you to my family for putting this incredible shindig together to celebrate my marriage to this wonderful woman on my right. And thank you to our friends for supporting us no matter what and for all of the presents I saw sitting on the foyer table." That got a laugh out of the crowd. "But in all seriousness, all I can really say is that my life is now complete with Kate and Calico in it. Thank you for coming tonight. We love you," Liam said. "Now, let's cut this damn cake!"

Chapter Fifteen

"That's the last of it." His brother Bruce stacked the last box in the moving van.

It was moving day for Liam, and several of his brothers had cleared their schedules so that they could help him move his life from Sugar Creek to the Triple K. It was a light move, considering that he was leaving most of his furniture behind. Kate didn't have room in her small ranch, and lately he'd been toying with the idea of renting out his cabin to people who wanted to experience life on a real Montana ranch. Of course, he was going to have to run that idea by Jock. Later.

"Are we ready to go?" Gabe, a long-distance hauler for high-end horses, had loaded both of his horses into the trailer.

"You can go on ahead," Liam told him. "Kate's waiting for you."

"All right, then." Gabe gave him a nod. "I'm moving out."

Bruce pulled down the door on the back of the van and locked it. "I'm heading out too."

"Thanks, man." Liam slapped his brother's shoulder. "Shane and I will be right behind you."

Shane, a veteran of the Iraq War, who rarely made an appearance at any family function, had managed to show for the move. Shane stood beside him quietly, his eyes red from lack of sleep and smoking too much dope.

"I think I'll cut out here," his brother said to him.

There was no sense pushing Shane. The war and too many deployments had changed him; he wasn't the same man who had left, and the family was beginning, slowly, to come to terms with the fact that he never would be again. This, the man that he was now, *was* Shane.

Liam hugged his brother. "Thanks for coming out to help, Shane. I know it's not easy for you."

"I like Kate," his brother said.

"I'm pretty partial to her myself."

After a short minute of silence, Shane changed the topic. "My landlady died."

"I'm sorry to hear that. When?"

Shane scratched his chin through his long, scraggly beard. "Oh, I don't know. About a month or two ago."

His brother seemed to be fuzzy with time a lot these days.

"No one's been around to collect rent. I may be kicked out of my place. Who knows. If I need a place to crash…?"

Liam cut him off. "No problem. You can stay here.

But no drugs, Shane. I don't want you smoking pot on my property."

Shane's lips turned up in the slightest of smiles. "I don't know what you're talkin' about, brother."

"Okay." Liam frowned, but gave his brother another hug for the road. "Sure you don't."

"I'm exhausted! I thought men traveled light!" Kate flopped onto their brand-new mattress after taking a long, hot, steamy shower. She had rifled through her husband's T-shirt drawer and was wearing one of his faded, black Trace Adkins concert shirts.

"It takes a lot of work to look this good." Liam raised one eyebrow and posed for her jokingly.

"Thank you. You do look good, I'll give you that."

Liam had his shirt off; he made his abs ripple for her. "Oh, yeah? Do you like what you see?"

"That's…amazing."

"If you're lucky, you can get some of this later," her husband said as he headed into the bathroom.

Kate listened to the sounds of Liam preparing for bed: turning on the faucet, brushing his teeth, uncapping the mouthwash. They had only been married a short while, and yet she had come to count on those sounds.

Liam appeared in the bathroom doorway naked as the day he was born; the man had never been shy about his nudity. And because the man preferred to sleep in the buff, Kate always checked their bedroom door to make sure it was locked. Callie knew better than to open a door without knocking, but she wasn't taking any chances.

Her husband turned off the lights but opened the

blinds so they could enjoy the light from the moon, as limited as it was. He climbed in bed beside her with a happy sigh.

"I have to admit." Kate turned her head toward him. "I don't miss the old mattress."

"I think you know where I stand on that topic." Liam reached for the remote control and clicked off the TV, which she had on mute.

Her husband leaned over, slipped his hand under her shirt, the palm of his hand on her stomach, his head resting on her thigh.

Kate began to rub his head, something she had discovered early on that he liked for her to do.

"Are you happy, Mrs. Brand?"

"Yes," she said on a sigh. She was happy. For the first time in a long time, she felt happy at her core. Oddly, she hadn't known that she was *unhappy* until she had a chance to know what it felt like to be loved by Liam.

"Are you?" she countered.

He kissed her thigh. "Yes. I am."

"Was it strange leaving Sugar Creek? I tried to imagine what it would be like to move away from here, and I couldn't."

"It was strange," he acknowledged. "A little sad. I never imagined my life anywhere else. Until now."

Kate's breath caught—she had been worried about Liam all day. How would he feel once he moved from his family's ranch? Would he genuinely feel that their marriage was worth that sacrifice? Much like the Triple K was to her, Sugar Creek was Liam's lifeblood. It was his heart.

"I'm sorry," she said.

"No." Liam lifted his head so he could look at her. "I

don't want you to apologize. I don't want you to worry
that I have any regrets, because I don't. Not one. *This* is
what I want. You. Callie. Our future here at the Triple
K. That's what matters to me. Yes, I was sad to leave
my home, but that sadness doesn't compare with the
happiness I feel being your husband."

Liam moved so he was next to her on the bed, so he
could take her into his arms and kiss her. They pressed
their bodies together, legs intertwined.

"I'm worried you're going to not like it here."

He looked into her eyes. "Hey. Listen to me, Kate.
I'm happy wherever you are."

Wanting to feel her naked flesh pressed against his,
Kate broke the embrace to take off her T-shirt and pant-
ies. She couldn't wait to get back into his arms.

"You feel good, baby." Liam kissed her neck.

"So do you."

He rolled her onto her back so he could kiss her between her thighs. He enjoyed loving her this way, and
she had gotten used to just *receiving* it. He kissed her
and licked her until she was squirming and tugging on
his arm to relieve the ache he had created.

"You taste as sweet as a sugar cookie." Liam covered her body with his.

She was so wet, so ready, that he slipped inside her
until he was so deep that it made her gasp. Liam looked
down at her, admiring her. He didn't move, not an inch.
Her husband loved to tease her, to toy with her in a
playful way.

"How do you want it, baby?" He nipped at her neck.

"Slow." She pushed her hips up against him. "Give
it to me slow."

Every inch of Liam's body gave her pleasure. He

loved her slowly, passionately, taking his time, massaging her breasts, kissing her lips, building her up until she was panting and straining and biting down on her lip to stop herself from making too much noise.

"Yes, baby."

Liam already knew her body so well that he could feel her getting ready to climax. She dug her nails into his back and bit down on his shoulder. Her orgasms with Liam were stronger, longer, more powerful than ever before. Usually Liam didn't come at the same time, but tonight, as she shuddered in his arms, her husband buried his face in her neck and groaned. She held on to him, holding him as he held her.

"Oh my God." Kate laughed quietly. "I hope it's always this good between us."

Liam separated their bodies and covered them both with the covers.

"It will be," he said with certainty. "We love each other."

Kate curled up with her back pressed against Liam's warm body. Her husband curled his body behind her like a spoon, his hand on her stomach.

"Good night, baby. Tomorrow is going to be a great day."

The day for the adoption had arrived. Tomorrow, Liam would legally become Callie's father. It would be the first time in her daughter's life that she truly had an active, loving father. And, for her, it would be the first time that she wasn't a single parent. Liam had come in, on his figurative white horse, and fixed parts of her life she didn't even realize were all that broken.

"I'm nervous," she admitted. "But so excited. Good night."

* * *

The lead up to this day had weighed on Liam heavily. Ever since it was in his heart to become Callie's father, knocking down all of the barriers in his way had become an obsession. The first hurdle was getting Lloyd to relinquish his parental rights, then he had to settle the back child support. Next, he needed to marry her mother—that wasn't a hurdle, it was a highlight. Now the final hurdle was about to be leaped—he would sit before the judge, answer questions posed by his attorney and Callie would be his.

"How do I look?" Kate was more nervous than he'd ever seen her before. "I don't know what happened. These pants shrunk, and now they look like high-waters."

"How about putting on your knee-high boots. I like those."

Her features were pinched, eyes worried. "Do you think they're appropriate?"

"Sure. Your feet are going to be under the table."

"Are you being serious or funny right now? If you're being funny, I don't appreciate it. I feel like we're running late."

"Come here, baby." Liam hugged her. "It's going to be okay. We aren't running late. You look great, as always. Just calm down. I'm right here, and everything's fine."

Kate wiggled free of the hug. "I don't even know why I feel so stressed out."

"Because—" he tried to reassure her "—this is a big deal. It's not every day your daughter gets adopted."

His wife disappeared into the closet.

"Any doubts?"

She came out with her knee-high boots in hand, dumped them on the floor and sat down on the bed so she could put them on.

"No." Kate stood and stomped her feet so her toes went down farther into the boots. "I don't have one single doubt. You are the best thing that's happened to Callie in a long time."

His wife came over and gave him a brief "apology" hug.

"I'm sorry I've been a bit off."

He rubbed her shoulders. "Don't worry about it. You're doing great."

Kate watched him carefully when she asked, "Do *you* have any doubts?"

He smiled at her. "Baby, I've got a few of best days in my life." He held up his fingers so he could count them as he went. "The day I graduated from vet school, the days my children were born, the day I married you and today."

They piled into Kate's truck, with him behind the wheel. Callie was with them, wearing a new dress just for the occasion. They had debated for quite a while about whether Callie should be in attendance; in the end, Kate didn't want this to be something that just "happened" to her daughter. It had taken weeks of preparation to get Callie to a place where she understood, on a basic level, what the adoption meant. Her first worry, which they expected, was that she already had a dad. But once they got Lloyd on the phone, and he assured her that he would always be her dad, and that nothing in the world would change that, Callie began the process of making sense of her changing reality.

Liam had to give Lloyd credit—the man had stepped

up, better late than never, and was acting in Callie's best interest.

"Do you remember why we're going to the courthouse today, Callie?" Kate looked over her shoulder into the backseat.

"Yes," Callie said with a smile. "Adoption."

"That's exactly right, kiddo." Her mother smiled back at her daughter. "Today you are going to get a bonus dad."

"Are you still good with that idea, Calico?" Liam glanced at his daughter-to-be in the review mirror.

"Yes." She nodded thoughtfully. "I—I like the i-idea."

"So do I." Kate put her hand on her husband's leg.

They arrived early and took a seat at the back of the courtroom. Callie sat between them, holding one of her mother's hands and one of Liam's. Callie didn't always understand the gravity or complexity of a situation, but she could feel the tension in their bodies, the anxiety in their voices, and now she was tense.

Liam looked over his shoulder every couple of minutes, anticipating his attorney's arrival. Finally, he saw Brad Williams walk through the door. He stood and shook the man's hand.

"Are we ready?" Liam asked, after Brad had taken a moment to greet Kate and Callie.

His attorney leaned forward and addressed all of them. "This is mainly procedural. The judge will swear you in, you'll spell your names for the record and state your address. We've got everything filed with the court. I don't anticipate any hiccups."

Liam tried to stop moving his leg up in down while they waited, but finally gave up. He wanted to be on the back end of this; he wanted Callie to be his daughter, legally and forever. When their case was called, all four of them moved to the table. Liam poured himself a glass of water, drank it and then poured another.

"Relax, Dad." Kate was now the one who appeared to be more at peace.

Judge Ackredge, a heavyset man with thick jowls, rounded nose and thick glasses, addressed the court, "We'll go on the record. This is docket 841-FA-029. Counsel."

When the judge wasn't in his robes, Charlie Ackredge was one of Liam's father's hunting and fishing buddies; it was nice to have a familiar face on the bench during the adoption hearing.

Brad stood for a second to address the judge. "Thank you, Your Honor. Brad Williams representing the petitioners."

The judge swore them in so they could proceed. Under the table, Liam held on to Kate's hand with a sweaty palm.

"Please answer the questions regarding the petition for adoption loud enough for the judge to hear." Brad took out the petition and turned to the signature page.

"Is the signature on the petition yours?"

"Yes."

"Were the facts in this petition true when you signed it?"

"Yes."

"Is the adult you want to adopt named Calico Kathryn King?"

"Yes."

The questions continued, one by one.

"Have you entered into a legal marriage with Kathryn Julia King?"

"Yes." Liam squeezed Kate's hand.

"Would you like there to be a name change?"

Liam looked at Callie to make sure she still wanted to become a Brand. Once Callie realized that her mother's name was Brand, she wanted to be a Brand, as well.

"Yes. Her name is Calico Kathryn King Brand."

It was a strong name; it was a good name.

Brad covered Liam's employment and his ability to support Callie, as well as letting him know that if the adoption was granted, that he would have the same rights and responsibilities as a parent or legal guardian. Which was exactly what he wanted.

The attorney then questioned Kate, asking her if she approved of the adoption by her husband of her daughter.

"Yes." Kate had tears in her eyes as she held on to his hand with both hands. "Yes, I do."

Next the attorney turned to Callie.

"Hi, Callie."

"Hi."

"I asked you earlier if it was okay if I asked you a few questions. Is it still okay?"

Callie nodded.

"Please say 'yes' if it's okay Callie," Brad prompted.

"Yes."

"Do you know why you're here, Callie?"

"To be adopted."

"And what does adoption mean to you?"

"I-it means that I'm going to b-be a part of the B-Brand family."

Brad nodded. "That's all I have, Your Honor."

Judge Ackredge took over the proceeding while Liam had to hold back tears. The last time he had cried was the day his divorce was final. This was a much better reason to have tears in his eyes.

"I have a properly completed petition for adoption for one adult. Based on the testimony I will enter a judgment of adoption today that will establish the same relationship between the dependent adult and the parent as if they had been born to the adoptive parent. Congratulations."

And that was that. After months of preparation and discussions and meetings with his attorney, Callie was *his* daughter.

"Congratulations." Brad shook his hand and then shook Kate's hand.

"Thank you so much," Kate said as she wiped tears from her cheeks. "For everything."

"It was my pleasure." The attorney gathered his belongings. "Congratulations, Callie."

Callie Brand ducked her head and giggled. "Thank you."

Outside the courthouse, Liam felt like a king. He was a husband to Kate and a father to Callie. Life was just about perfect.

"Brand family hug!" Liam opened his arms wide.

Kate and Callie stepped into his arms, and they all hugged each other.

After they broke the hug, Liam addressed his daughter. He put his hands on her shoulders.

"You're my daughter now, Callie. Forever."

His daughter rewarded him with a wide smile.

"You can't call me Dr. Brand anymore," he told her. "What do you want to call me?"

"I—I don't know."

Kate put her arm around Callie's shoulder. "You

already have a 'Daddy.' How about if you call Liam 'Dad'?"

Callie threw herself back into his arms and hugged him. "Dad."

For the last hour, Liam had been holding back tears. When Callie called him "Dad," he didn't even try to hold them back any longer.

Kate wrapped her arms around both of them for a second group hug. She caught Liam's eyes and mouthed, *Thank you*.

"We're a family," Liam said as they headed back to the truck. "Now and for the rest of our lives."

Chapter Sixteen

"Are you all packed?" Kate stood in the doorway of her daughter's room.

This was a day that Kate had been dreading; this was the day that she flew with Callie to San Diego. Liam had offered to travel with them, but she felt that this was something she needed to do on her own. Perhaps it didn't seem like a monumental step for her from the outside looking in; for her, this was a rite of passage for Callie. Her daughter had never been out of state for a day, much less two weeks, without her.

"I—I'm ready to go!" Callie pulled her heavy suitcase off her bed, and it hit the ground with a thud.

"You aren't going there forever, Callie," Kate reminded her daughter. "You're coming back in two weeks."

"I—I know. I—I need to have options."

That made Kate laugh. "Fair enough, kiddo."

Callie had certainly packed options; Kate had been with her daughter to make sure she had packed all essentials, while her fashionista daughter had focused on her wardrobe. Wherever Callie had gotten her sense of style, it hadn't come from Kate.

Callie happily wheeled her suitcase out of the room, past her mother and stopped at the door.

"All right." Kate grabbed her keys off the counter. "Let's go before I lose my nerve."

They would be flying to San Diego with one stop in Salt Lake City. It would take them nearly four hours of fly time and six hours total. Callie didn't like to fly, which hadn't dampened her enthusiasm for the trip… yet. It would, though. Liam insisted on buying first-class seats in order to make the trip easier on the both of them. She resisted in the beginning, but couldn't deny his logic after a couple rounds of discussions between them. Having the extra room, having Callie close to a bathroom, would make the trip go much more smoothly overall.

"Are you all checked in?" Liam asked her when she called him from the airport.

"All checked in," she confirmed. "Callie's anxiety has already started to crack through her excitement."

"Just be careful. I believe in you and I believe in Callie."

They exchanged I-love-yous, and then soon after that phone call, first class was given priority boarding onto the plane. Normally Kate liked to be one of the last on the plane—she wasn't a fan of flying either. But today she took advantage of the perk and used the extra time to get Callie settled in the seat next to the window.

By the time all passengers had boarded, Callie had a ginger ale, called Tony before Kate showed her how to put her phone in airplane mode, and accepted a pillow and blanket from the steward. Callie was snuggled beneath her blanket, looking out the window, when the cabin door was slammed shut. Her daughter jumped, her face registering that familiar panic.

Kate reached for her daughter's hand. "We're going to push back from the gate, Callie. First we'll get in line at the runway for takeoff."

"And then we take off."

"Just close your eyes and hold on to my hand, kiddo. Think about how happy you'll be when you see Tony at the airport."

This garnered a small, nervous smile from Callie. "I—I can do it, Mommy."

"Calico, I know you can."

We are here.

Kate sent a text to Liam the moment they landed in San Diego. She had to admit to herself that she had underestimated her daughter. Callie was growing up, and she was highly motivated to see Tony, and this new maturity and motivation made the trip go much easier than Kate had imagined.

"Do you see them?" Callie had asked this question several times as they deplaned.

"Are we at baggage claim yet?"

"No."

"Where are they going to pick us up?"

"B-baggage claim."

"So, what do you think?"

Callie giggled at herself. "They're at b-baggage claim!"

And they were at baggage claim; Tony, his mother and his father were all awaiting their arrival. Tony was armed with balloons, flowers and a large stuffed bear.

"Hi," Kate greeted Tony's parents while Callie hugged her boyfriend.

Tottie ignored her offered hand and hugged her; she smelled sweet, like candy. Tony Sr. refrained from hugging her, for which she was grateful.

"Callie!" Kate called out to her daughter who was kissing Tony right there in baggage claim. "You need to come and watch out for your bag."

"Young love," Tottie said, her body language saying that she was just as uncomfortable as she was about the kissing in public.

Kate was lucky to get a flight back to Bozeman within a couple hours of landing. The Salvianos took her out for an early dinner, which gave her an opportunity to go over Callie's health concerns and diet restrictions. Tony and Callie sat at a separate table; every now and again, Kate would watch her daughter sitting with her boyfriend. It was hard to admit, it was hard to process, but she could easily see that Tony was smitten with Callie.

The return trip was a tiring, long and lonely event for Kate. She had never left her daughter in another state with virtual strangers. Every fiber of her being railed against it. Yet it's what she had to do. She had to let Callie go. All her life, she had told Callie that she could do anything, be anything. Now those chickens had come home to roost, because her daughter was putting those words into action.

She had a heavy heart when she landed in Bozeman, feeling so worn down that she thought about taking a nap in her truck before making the trip home. Kate sent Liam a text the moment the plane landed; he answered back that he would see her when she got home.

"Hello, Mrs. Brand."

Kate was startled when she heard her husband's voice where she hadn't expected to hear it. There, leaning against a pillar just outside the airport entrance, was Liam.

"What are you doing here?" she asked, but didn't wait for him to answer before she threw her arms around him and buried her head in his chest.

"Waiting for my lovely wife." He ran his hand gently over her hair, holding her tight.

Unbidden, tears that she had been holding back for hours, days, weeks, poured out of her eyes and onto his shirt.

"It's okay," Liam said quietly. "Everything is going to be okay. Let's go home."

Liam had gotten his brother to drop him off at the airport so he could drive her back to the Triple K. It was, by far, the sweetest, and to her, the most romantic gesture a man had ever made to her.

In the passenger seat, Kate leaned back, closed her eyes and periodically wiped the tears off her cheeks.

"I can't believe you're here," she said, her voice choked with emotion.

"I knew this was going to be a tough one for you." Liam shifted into gear and started the journey home.

Kate opened her eyes, put her hand on his leg. "Thank you."

"You're welcome, baby. This is part of my job."

* * *

It had been only two days since he had picked Kate up from the airport, and now he was back to pick up his daughter Sarah. It took some doing, some negotiating with her mother, but eventually his ex approved the unscheduled trip. Liam suspected that his teenage daughter, who took after the Brand side of her family, was making her mother's life hell.

"Hi, Dad." Sarah had her bangs in her eyes and a mopey look on her face.

"Hi." He hugged her tightly even though she tried to resist. "I'm glad to see you."

They gathered her bags and headed out. Liam tried, mostly unsuccessfully, to pry some sort of conversation out of his daughter. There was one subject she *did* want to talk to him about.

"I want to stay at Sugar Creek."

"We'll visit." He told her the same thing he told her on the phone. "But I don't live there anymore, Sarah. I live at Triple K Ranch. With my wife."

That stopped all communication until he turned into the long winding drive that led to the Triple K homestead.

"Look at this place, Sarah. As far as the eye can see. You can ride for miles and never find a fence."

Sarah stared out the passenger window. "It's not as pretty as Sugar Creek."

"Sugar Creek is God's country," Liam agreed. "But so is Triple K."

"She *hates* me," Kate whispered while they were brushing their teeth. It was her idea to bring Sarah on their stay-at-home honeymoon, but it was a suggestion that she seriously regretted. From the moment Sarah arrived at the Triple K, the teenager was a nonstop stream of complaints, "remember when Mom and you did" comments and negativity aimed at everything Triple K Ranch.

Liam didn't deny it because he *couldn't* deny it.

Her husband spit toothpaste into the sink, and turned on the water to rinse out his mouth and wash the toothpaste down the drain.

"She acts like she hates you. But I don't think she does. Not really."

Sarah was bunking in Callie's room; already she had complaints about the mattress and the low ceilings and the fact that there wasn't a bathroom attached.

"No," she argued. "She really hates me. It's like she's been waiting for you to get back together with her mom, even though her mom is *remarried*, and I've come along and screwed everything up!"

Kate yanked back the covers, frustrated. She punched her pillows with her fist, then got into bed, kicking her feet to loosen the sheets tucked in tightly at the end of the mattress.

Liam joined her in bed. It was the first time since they had married that they were disagreeing. It didn't feel good.

"I'm telling you, I know Sarah. She doesn't hate you. She's angry with me, she's angry with her mother..."

"And I'm an easy target," Kate snapped. "Does she even know that I'm the reason she's here? That I wanted her to be with us on our honeymoon?"

"I've told her, baby." Liam turned off the light to signal he was ready to go to bed.

Still sitting upright, and annoyed Liam was shutting

her down by shutting off the light, Kate stared into the darkened room.

"Hey…" Her husband touched her arm. "Come on. Lay down. She's only been here for one night."

Kate looked at Liam. She was tired, he was tired. Maybe she should just drop the conversation and see what the next day would bring.

She scooted down in bed, flipped away from him so her back was to him and pulled the covers over her shoulder.

"Hey…" Liam leaned over for his good-night kiss. "Where are you."

"I'm right here." Kate turned her head enough to accept the kiss.

Liam gave her a quick kiss and then lay back down. "Good night, baby. I love you."

"Good night."

Then, after a minute of silence, she added, "I love you, too."

The Triple K was a big enough ranch for both of them. This was what Kate thought after she left the house after breakfast, with a still moody and unhappy Sarah sitting at the kitchen table. The only thing she could do, the only thing she had control over, was work. There were horses to train, so she decided to get to it.

A beautiful Friesian, a muscular, coal black horse with feathered hooves, had been delivered to the Triple K for training. Kate had been itching to take him for a ride, but first she wanted to earn his respect on the ground.

"Come on, Solomon." Kate led the powerful gelding out of his stall.

She started working with Solomon in the round pen, without a halter or bridle. Kate stood in the center of the ring, putting the Friesian through his paces. First she had him walk, then trot, and then canter to the left and then to the right.

"Good boy." She walked up beside him, gave him a treat from her pocket and then moved him forward by swinging the rope in the direction of his hindquarters.

"Who's this?" Liam asked, hanging over the top rail of the round pen.

"Solomon," Kate said, not taking her eyes off the gelding trotting around the edge of the pen. "Isn't he spectacular?"

"He certainly is," her husband agreed. "I've got to run into town, get a couple of things from the store. Sarah doesn't want to come with me. Is it okay with you if she stays here?"

Honestly, she wished Sarah would go with her father. But that wasn't realistic. She had invited her step-daughter to the ranch to get to know her—Kate was the adult, and it was her job to break through the attitude and connect with Sarah. She couldn't do that if she was always sending her off with Liam.

"That's fine." Kate nodded. "We'll be fine."

She finished working with Solomon and moved on to the next horse on her list for training. Riding boarded horses, keeping them exercised and making sure they picked up their cues to trot or canter, was a big part of how she made a living.

"What's his name?"

Sarah had been watching her work with the Friesian from across the yard. She hadn't gotten too close to the round pen, but the teen's interest in her work with horses seemed like a possibility to make a connection.

"Solomon."

Sarah pushed away from the wall, her features so like her father's, that the teen tugged at her heart.

"Can I ride him?"

"Not this one." Kate handed Solomon's lead to one of the stable hands. "Rinse him off, cool him down and then turn him out in the north pasture.

"I don't own him." Kate finished answering Sarah's question. "I can show you the horses you can ride. Your father's horses are here too."

That was when Kate first saw a spark in Sarah, a point of connection. She could work with this. Kate saddled up one of her horses and let Sarah ride. The girl had a great seat in the saddle, and Kate told her so over lunch.

"I rode all the time when I lived at Sugar Creek," Liam's daughter reminded her. "I don't get to ride in Seattle. Ever."

The conversation ended there. Kate had never been one to beat around the bush, and she had a feeling that Sarah was someone who appreciated cutting to the chase.

"You don't like me," she said.

Sarah stopped chewing, looked up at her, surprise in those bright blue eyes so like Liam's own bright blue eyes.

"No."

"Because I married your dad?"

Sarah shook her head. "No. I don't care about that anymore."

Kate raised an eyebrow and waited.

"I don't know." The teen frowned into her plate.

"I know you want to move back to Montana," Kate said. "Do you think now that your father is married to me that you can't move back to Montana?"

A shrug was all she got, but Kate knew, instinctively, that this the reason behind a big chunk of the resentment Sarah was feeling toward her.

"Are you finished?" she asked the teen.

A nod.

"Help me clear the table. I want to show you something."

After they cleared the table, Kate rolled out the new house plans on the table for Sarah to see.

"This is the house your father and I are going to build."

Sarah tried to act like she wasn't interested; Kate could see that she was.

The horse trainer pointed to one of the rooms in the house. "Do you know what this is?"

A shake of the head. "Nope."

"*This* is your room."

That got the teen's attention. "My room?"

"That's right," Kate said. "Your father and I want you to have a place with us. I can't guarantee that we can get your mom to agree to let you live with us full time. But we are going to try."

Sarah stared at her, unblinking, and then ran her finger over her bedroom on the house plans.

"We want you to be with us, Sarah," Kate said. "Do you understand? Triple K is your home too."

Liam wasn't sure what he was going to find when he arrived back at the ranch. He had hoped that Sarah and Kate would find some common ground upon which to build a relationship if he gave them some space and time.

He expected to find Sarah holed up in Callie's room on her computer and Kate in the barn with her horses. He did not expect to see the two of them, standing at the top of the hill where they were going to build their dream home.

Liam shifted into Park, turned off the truck and leaned forward so he could get a better look out the windshield.

He wasn't imagining it—his daughter and his wife were standing together on the site where they planned on breaking ground in a month.

"What's going on up here?" Liam had decided to leave his truck parked and hike up the hill.

"Hi!" Kate had a genuine, easy smile on her face. "We're making plans for the new house."

"Kate says I can paint my room any color I want."

"Other than black," Kate corrected.

"Other than black," Sarah amended.

Kate put her arms around his waist, kissed him quickly and then said, "I hope you don't mind that I ruined the surprise. I showed Sarah the house plans."

"What do you think?" he asked his daughter, whose face had lost its scowl.

Sarah gave a little nod. "It's pretty cool."

"Yeah," Liam agreed. "It is pretty cool."

His daughter kicked a clump of dirt, walking in a circle where her room would eventually be.

She stopped, looked at him directly in the eye and asked, "Are you really going to try to get mom to let me live with you?"

Liam caught Kate's eye; he understood why she had talked to Sarah about this before he'd had the chance. The timing was right, and she did it. If it helped heal their relationship, then he was glad.

"Come here." He held out his free arm; when she reached his side, he put his arm around her shoulders. "Do you know what I know about your mom?" Liam asked his daughter. "I know that your mom loves you more than anything else in her life."

Sarah frowned at him, but he persisted.

"It's true, Sarah. And if your mom thinks that it's best for you to live here full-time, or at least for the summer, she'll say yes. And I'm going to give convincing her one heck of shot, Sarah. That's what I can promise. Can you live with that?"

His daughter nodded, and for the first time in a long time, Sarah leaned against him and put her head on his shoulder.

"It's going to be another beautiful day." Liam gazed out at the clear, blue Montana sky.

Standing there with his wife and his younger daughter at his side, Liam realized that all of his wishes had been granted. He was a husband, a father; he was building a home with the woman he loved; one day, they would be surrounded by their children and grandchildren. He finally had a family of his own. Perhaps he didn't deserve it, but God had, indeed, been good to Liam Brand.

* * * * *

*If you loved this story,
be sure to look for the next book in*
THE BRANDS OF MONTANA *series,
available August 2018
from Harlequin Special Edition!*

*And in the meantime, check out these other
emotional romances by Joanna Sims:*

*A WEDDING TO REMEMBER
THANKFUL FOR YOU
MEET ME AT THE CHAPEL
HIGH COUNTRY BABY*

*Available now wherever
Harlequin books and ebooks are sold!*

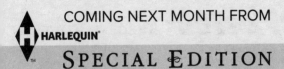

COMING NEXT MONTH FROM
HARLEQUIN®
SPECIAL EDITION

Available February 20, 2018

#2605 THE FORTUNE MOST LIKELY TO...
The Fortunes of Texas: The Rulebreakers • by Marie Ferrarella
Everett Fortunado has never quite gotten over his high school love, Lila Clark.
So when circumstance offers him a second chance, he grabs it. But is Lila
willing to forget their past and risk her heart on a millionaire doctor with ties to
the Fortunes?

#2606 THE SHERIFF'S NINE-MONTH SURPRISE
Match Made in Haven • by Brenda Harlen
After a weekend of shared passion, Katelyn Gilmore doesn't expect to see
Reid Davidson again—until she meets Haven's new sheriff! But she has a
surprise, too—scheduled to arrive in nine months...

#2607 A PROPOSAL FOR THE OFFICER
American Heroes • by Christy Jeffries
Fighter pilot Molly Markham is used to navigating her own course. Billionaire
Kaleb Chatterson has never found a problem he couldn't fix. But when the two
pretend to be in a fake relationship to throw off their families, neither one has
control over their own hearts.

#2608 THE BEST MAN TAKES A BRIDE
Hillcrest House • by Stacy Connelly
Best man Jamison Porter doesn't believe in a love of a lifetime. But will his
daughter's adoration of sweet—and sexy—wedding planner Rory McClaren
change this cynical lawyer's mind about finding a new happily-ever-after?

#2609 FOREVER A FATHER
The Delaneys of Sandpiper Beach • by Lynne Marshall
After a devastating loss, Daniel Delaney just wants to be left alone with his grief
and his work. But his new employee, the lovely Keela O'Mara, and her daughter
might be just the people to help remind him that love—and family—can make
life worth living again.

#2610 FROM EXES TO EXPECTING
Sutter Creek, Montana • by Laurel Greer
When Tavish Fitzgerald, a globe-trotting photojournalist, gets stuck in Montana
for a family wedding, one last night with Lauren Dawson, his hometown doctor
ex-wife, leads them from exes to expecting—and finally tempts him to stay put!

**YOU CAN FIND MORE INFORMATION ON UPCOMING HARLEQUIN® TITLES,
FREE EXCERPTS AND MORE AT WWW.HARLEQUIN.COM.**

HSECNM0218

Everett Fortunado never got over his high school love, Lila Clark. So when circumstance offers him a second chance, he grabs it with both hands. But is Lila willing to forget their past and risk her heart on a millionaire doctor with ties to the Fortunes?

Read on for a sneak preview of
THE FORTUNE MOST LIKELY TO...
by USA TODAY bestselling author
Marie Ferrarella, *the next installment in*
THE FORTUNES OF TEXAS:
THE RULEBREAKERS *continuity.*

Before Lila could ask any more questions, she suddenly found herself looking up at Everett. The fund-raiser was a black-tie affair and Everett was wearing the obligatory tuxedo.

It was at that moment that Lila realized Everett in a tuxedo was even more irresistible than Everett wearing scrubs.

Face it, the man would be irresistible even wearing a kilt.

"What are you doing here?" Lila asked when she finally located her tongue and remembered how to use it.

"You know, we're going to have to work on getting you a new opening line to say every time you see me," Everett told her with a laugh. "But to answer your question, I was invited."

Lucie stepped up with a slightly more detailed explanation to her friend's question. "The invitation was the foundation's way of saying thank you to Everett for his volunteer work."

"Disappointed to see me?" he asked Lila. There was a touch of humor in his voice, although he wasn't quite sure just what to make of the stunned expression on Lila's face.

"No, of course not," Lila denied quickly. "I'm just surprised, that's all. I thought you were still back in Houston."

"I was," Everett confirmed. "The invitation was express mailed to me yesterday. I thought it would be rude to ignore it, so here I am," he told her simply, as if all he had to do was teleport himself from one location to another instead of drive over one hundred and seventy miles.

"Here you are," Lila echoed.

Everything inside her was smiling and she knew that was a dangerous thing. Because when she was in that sort of frame of mind, she tended not to be careful. And that was when mistakes were made.

Mistakes with consequences.

She was going to have to be on her guard, Lila silently warned herself. And it wasn't going to be easy being vigilant, not when Everett looked absolutely bone-meltingly gorgeous the way he did.

As if his dark looks weren't already enough, Lila thought, the tuxedo made Everett look particularly dashing.

You're not eighteen anymore, remember? Lila reminded herself. *You're a woman. A woman who has to be very, very careful.*

She just hoped she could remember that.

Don't miss
THE FORTUNE MOST LIKELY TO...
by Marie Ferrarella, available March 2018 wherever
Harlequin® Special Edition books and ebooks are sold.

www.Harlequin.com

LOVE
Harlequin
romance?

Join our Harlequin community to share your thoughts and connect with other romance readers!

Be the first to find out about promotions, news, and exclusive content!

Sign up for the Harlequin e-newsletter and download a free book from any series at

www.TryHarlequin.com

CONNECT WITH US AT:

Harlequin.com/Community

 Facebook.com/HarlequinBooks

 Twitter.com/HarlequinBooks

 Instagram.com/HarlequinBooks

 Pinterest.com/HarlequinBooks

ReaderService.com

**ROMANCE WHEN
YOU NEED IT**

HSOCIAL2017